Arson Old Lace and Murder

A Charlie Kingsley Mystery

Books and series by Michele Pariza Wacek

Charlie Kingsley Mysteries
(Cozy Mysteries)
See all of Charlie's adventures here.
https://MPWnovels.com/r/ck_aom

Redemption Detective Agency
(Cozy Mysteries)
A spin-off from the Charlie Kingsley series.
https://MPWNovels.com/r/da_aom

Secrets of Redemption series
(Pychological Thrillers)
The flagship series that started it all.
https://MPWnovels.com/r/rd_aom

Mysteries of Redemption
(Psychological Thrillers)
A spin-off from the Secrets of Redemption series
https://MPWnovels.com/r/mr_aom

Riverview Mysteries
(standalone Pychological Thrillers)
These stories take place in Riverview, which is
near
Redemption.
https://MPWnovels.com/r/rm_aom

Arson Old Lace and Murder

A Charlie Kingsley Mystery

by Michele Pariza Wacek

For my family, for always believing in me.

Chapter 1

It started with the smell of smoke.

I was getting in my car when I first noticed it—the unmistakable scent of burning wood. It was strong enough to cause me to pause and look around, my breath transforming into puffs of white steam in the sharp, wintery air.

Could it be from someone's fireplace? It seemed too excessive for that, especially since I didn't see any smoke coming from any of the nearby chimneys. But what other explanation was there? No one would be having a bonfire; Wisconsin in late January was way too cold. Not to mention the piles and piles of dirty snow and pockets of ice as far as the eye could see. Who the heck would want to be outside in all of that?

Although … on second thought, this area of Redemption *was* considered strange by the townspeople. While technically, it was still within the town's limits (albeit barely), in reality, it was more like another world. Redemption was too small to have suburbs, but if it wasn't, I suspected this area would have been it. In so many ways, it felt completely different from Redemption proper, and it didn't help that many of its residents rarely, if ever, came into town. And vice versa.

Despite that, I did have one tea client who lived here. Hattie, an elderly woman, was basically housebound. She never really went outside anymore, especially this time of year. The cold made her arthritis flare up even more than usual. She swore my tea was the only thing that helped her manage her pain and insomnia, and I was more than happy to do a monthly drop-off of her order, which was why I was in the neighborhood this cold, gray afternoon.

I supposed it was possible someone, somewhere was having a bonfire, as unlikely as it seemed. Either way, I figured it didn't warrant my concern. Even if there was a little niggle at the back of my head indicating something was wrong.

I ignored it and got into my car. I still had a number of deliveries to make before the end of the day, and the sooner I finished, the sooner I would be back in my warm kitchen with a hot cup of tea and a homemade chocolate chip cookie. Or maybe two. Actually, on second thought, I was almost out of cookies. Maybe I would make another batch tonight. That would be a perfect way to spend a cold, January evening in Wisconsin.

I was so busy dreaming about filling my house with the tantalizing scents of warm, baking cookies, I almost missed the fire.

I was about to turn right, which would take me back to Redemption proper, when I spotted the black smoke billowing out from my left. I braked, staring into the growing cloud. It looked *big*. Much too big to be a bonfire even.

Before I could think about it too much, I flipped the turn signal on the left and started toward the fire. It might be nothing … but it also might be something. Someone's house could be burning down, and they might need all the help they could get.

The street I was on was considered the "business" section of the strange little community. I passed a gas station with an oversized convenience store, which was where most of the residents shopped for the majority of their staples (despite being less than ten minutes away from a huge grocery store that I was sure would have a much bigger selection and probably better prices). There was also a local drugstore, a diner, and a couple of bars, at least one of which served food. Even though it was the middle of the day, the entire block seemed completely deserted—no one else was on the road, and I saw only a couple of cars parked near the businesses. If I hadn't known better, I would have thought I was driving through a ghost town.

The smoke grew thicker and thicker as I drove, and the uneasy feeling in the pit of my stomach intensified. I was at least a couple of blocks away from the origin, but I was even more sure it was a house fire. I was just starting to see the orange-red flames licking the bottom of the smoke when I knew for sure it was going to be bad. I could feel it.

And where was everyone? As far as I could tell, no one was around. Nor could I hear the sound of sirens, even from afar. Did that mean no one had called the fire department yet? Finding a phone was also a priority.

In a small alley to my right, which was lined with warehouses and machine shops, thick, black smoke billowed. It had to be the source of the fire, and it looked bad. I turned into the alley and quickly sped up.

That's when I realized it wasn't exactly an alley, but more of a short, dead-end road. At the end of it, tucked behind a huge parking lot, was a large wooden structure … being consumed by flames.

I slammed on my brakes, fishtailing on the gravel road before parking where the road ran out and turned into a dirty-looking field peppered with a few sad trees. I jumped out of the car and ran toward the structure. The fire was so massive, I couldn't really tell what it originally was anymore. I was sure it had to be some sort of business establishment, though. I could still make out the remains of a large sign on the wooden, wraparound porch. Squinting, I could just barely make out the letters … something like 88 Spir, whatever that meant.

The heat was intense on my face, and the smoke seemed to coat the inside of my nose and throat. I coughed and put my hand out to try to shield my face, like that would do anything, as I peered around for anyone who might be trapped or in need of help. The sound of crackling wood and the whooshing of the flames was so loud, I wasn't sure I would even be able to hear someone over it.

I started to circle around to the back of the building, keeping my mouth and nose covered with my gloved hand, which did nothing for my coughing.

"Help!"

The sound was so feeble that for a moment, I thought I'd imagined it, but then, I saw it. A distorted face pressed against the glass of a small, dirty window that had been shoved open. A pale hand was pounding on the glass.

I ran as fast as I could in my winter boots, skittering on the snow-packed cement. "What can I do? Are you trapped? Do you need me to help you out the window?"

A wild eye focused on me. The surrounding face was smeared with soot, but it was clearly female. "Not the window. I'll never fit."

Never fit? While it was true I couldn't see her entire body, what I could see looked petite and delicate. "Are you trapped? I can come get you."

"No!" Her voice was nearly a scream. "Don't come in! The ceiling is going to cave. Just get the back door open." She started pointing furiously to my left.

"No problem," I yelled and started running alongside the building, searching for the door and praying it wouldn't be covered in flames.

Luckily, it wasn't, but I could immediately see why it wouldn't open. There was a large piece of wood wedged under the doorknob. I kicked it aside and wrenched open the door.

Hot air and smoke poured out, and I covered my face with my arm, trying not to cough too much as I leaned inside to find the girl. She was already making her way toward me, waddling awkwardly between chairs and tables. I could immediately see why she said she would never fit through the window. Her large breasts and massive stomach would definitely be impediments. I also couldn't help but notice she wasn't dressed for the time of year. Rather than wearing a sweatshirt or sweater, she wore what seemed to be a thin smock with sleeves that were shoved up above her elbows. She must have removed some items of clothing at some point during the fire, but I wished she hadn't. She was in for a shock once she stepped outside.

She stumbled as she neared the door, and I quickly jumped in to steady her. The heat was like a furnace. Beads of sweat dotted my forehead, and I quickly realized I had been too hasty in my judgment of her lack of clothing. Regardless, from what I could see, the rest of the building was an inferno. If this girl hadn't been so close to the window, there was no way I would have been able to find her.

I grabbed her arm and pulled her out into the cold, gray air. She was coughing so hard, she was practically doubled over, and I put an arm around her as I helped her away from the building.

"Are you hurt?" I asked.

She was still coughing but managed to shake her head, although that didn't really reassure me.

"We should get you checked out," I said, leading her to my car. Where was the fire department? I was just about to drive her to the hospital myself when she stopped me.

She reared back so suddenly that my arm wrenched backward, too, and she stared at me intensely. "No ... no doctor ..." she gasped. Tears were streaming down her cheeks, leaving wet trails in the soot covering her face. I noticed two things then: one, she was much younger than I'd thought, and prettier.

And second, she wasn't overweight. She was pregnant.

"Oh no," I said firmly. "You and the baby absolutely need to be checked out."

She shook her head frantically, trying unsuccessfully to stop herself from coughing. "No! No ... doctor. I'm ... I'm ... fine. It's ... Arth ... Arth ..."

"Arth?" I couldn't figure out what she was trying to say.

She shook her head again, this time more out of frustration. "Arthur. He ... he's still ... he's still ..." she gestured with her head toward the burning building.

My eyes went wide. "Wait, you're saying someone is still inside?"

She nodded, her eyes wet with tears as she stared at me. "But ... you can't ... the ceiling ..." she started coughing again. Her entire body started shaking, although whether from cold or adrenaline, I wasn't sure.

"Okay, first things first," I said, taking off my very nice, and very warm, winter coat and wrapping it around the girl. Immediately, I felt the wind slice through my clothes. I may as well have been naked, as the turtleneck, sweater, and jeans did nothing to ward off the cold. I knew I had a hooded sweatshirt in the car, which wouldn't be as nice as my winter coat, but at least then, the cold wouldn't kill me when I came back to look for Arthur. Although, based on what I was seeing, I wasn't holding a lot of hope for finding him if he was still in the middle of the blaze. "I'm taking you to my car, and then I'll come back for Arthur."

Her eyes were wild. "No ... no, you can't ... the ceiling ..."

"Let me worry about the ceiling," I said grimly. "Now, let's get you back to my car."

She looked like she wanted to protest more, but I could also tell she wasn't in any condition to. As I led her around the building, I glanced back at the door, my heart sinking into my stomach. I couldn't imagine Arthur had survived, but maybe he had managed to get out and was somewhere close by, possibly hurt or unable to breathe. I had to at least look for him, even if I knew there was no way I could get back into the building myself. Maybe the firefighters would finally appear by then, and one of them could attempt a rescue.

But as much as I wanted to help Arthur, whoever he was, my biggest concern was the pregnant girl I was half-carrying, half-dragging to my car. I didn't understand why she was so adamant about not seeing a doctor; hopefully, it was just a reaction to the stress and insanity of what she had just experienced. The bottom line was that she absolutely needed to be checked out. I couldn't imagine breathing in all that smoke was good for her or the baby.

"I'm Charlie," I said, hoping she would volunteer her name. But before she could answer, she started coughing again, so I didn't press it.

We reached the car, and I let go of her to unlock the passenger side and bundle her in, tossing my purse into the backseat, which was also where I kept my spare hooded sweatshirt. Throwing it on, I looked at her. "Stay here," I ordered as I slammed the door and ran around to put the keys in the ignition, so I could start the car and get the heater running. She was trembling uncontrollably now, even with my nice winter jacket, along with the coughing. Man, the coughing couldn't be good for the baby. I really had to convince her to see a doctor.

I slid into the driver's seat and started the car, cranking the heat up to high. "I'll be right back," I said, turning to face her. Despite her huge belly, she seemed so small and so fragile, and my heart broke a little. "I'm going to see if I can find your friend. Arthur, is it?"

Her eyes went wide again, and she shook her head. "No ... no ... you can't. The ceiling ..." she repeated.

"I'm not going to endanger myself," I said, trying to reassure her. "I'm just going to look around and see if I can find him. Maybe he got out, like you did."

She looked at me, and there was such sadness, such despair in her eyes, my heart sank even further, though I didn't think that was possible. "No, I don't think so …"

"Well, we can hope, can't we?" I said, forcing myself to sound more optimistic than I felt. "You'll be fine here for a few minutes?"

She looked around hesitantly before nodding.

"Great," I said, sliding out of the car. I didn't really want to leave her, but I also knew I had to at least see if I could help Arthur. Plus, I needed to find a phone. There had to be one somewhere close by.

I had just circled the burning building when I heard the distinct sound of sirens. Finally! At least I didn't need to worry about a phone anymore. Now, it was just Arthur and the girl. Although it occurred to me that I had left a perfect stranger in my car with the keys in the ignition. What was to stop her from driving away? And I didn't even know her name.

An image of her flashed in my mind, with her soot-streaked face, bloodshot eyes, and constant coughing. Even if she did try to drive away, I didn't think she was going to get far.

Regardless, I found myself quickening my steps as I headed back around the building. I told myself it didn't make much sense for me to be out there anyway, now that the firefighters were on their way. I could let them worry about Arthur while I took care of the girl.

I reached the front of the building at the same time the fire truck pulled up to the curb. To my relief, I also saw my car, still idling where I'd left it.

One of the firefighters was heading toward me. "Are you hurt?" he called out as he approached. He was good-looking in a wholesome, clean-cut way, with close-cropped brown hair under his firefighter's helmet, dark-brown eyes, and chiseled features. He wore the long, yellow jacket typical of firefighters, and his ID, printed with the name Max, bounced against his chest.

I shook my head. "I'm fine. I wasn't in the building. But I think there might be someone still in there."

Max's eyes widened as he glanced at the fire, swearing under his breath as he turned to gesture toward the other firemen who were busy unwinding the hose from the truck. "Hey, we got a …"

Crack. The sound of the roof collapsing interrupted whatever he was going to say. We both turned to look at what was left of the building.

"I don't think there's anything we can do," he said. "You sure there was someone in there?"

"No," I admitted. "That's what the other survivor told me."

His gaze sharpened. "A survivor? Where is he?"

"She," I said, nodding toward my car. "In my car. She's pregnant."

"Pregnant?" He immediately turned and started waving toward the paramedics, who had arrived in an ambulance behind the firetruck.

"Hold on," I said, grabbing his arm. "She's young. And skittish. I wanted her to get some medical attention, but she refused. So we'll need to be … gentle in our approach."

He eyed me but gave me a quick nod before jogging over to the paramedics, who were in the process of removing the stretcher. At the same time, the other firefighters had finished getting the hose hooked up and turned on the water, which was now streaming onto the fire.

After exchanging a few words with the paramedic, Max waved at me and headed toward my car, his long legs making meaningful strides against the dirty snow. I had to practically run to catch up, which was awkward in my winter boots. Luckily, he saw me struggling and slowed down a bit.

"She needs to get checked out," he said once I reached him. "Do you think you can convince her?"

"I can try," I said.

He flashed me a quick, sideways smile. "I have faith in you."

I smiled back, although I wasn't nearly as confident. I could still see the panic and desperation in her eyes. Hopefully, it was just a temporary reaction to the adrenaline coursing through her body. If it wasn't … well, I would cross that bridge when I got to it.

As we drew nearer to my car, I suddenly realized I couldn't see her anymore. Had she collapsed? I broke into a half-run, kicking myself for not insisting on getting her medical attention sooner.

Max glanced at me, raising an eyebrow in question as he quickened his own pace, but I was too focused on trying to find her to answer. He followed my gaze, and I heard him inhale sharply. "I thought you said you left her in the car?"

"I did," I said as I finally reached the passenger door. I peered into the window, sure I was going to see her slumped forward, maybe unconscious, but the seat was empty. I quickly looked at the back seat, thinking maybe she was lying down, but I didn't see her there either.

"Oh no," I said, flinging open the passenger door as if she had somehow managed to shrink down and hide in the crevices. But deep down, I knew it was useless.

The car was empty.

She was gone.

Chapter 2

It wasn't just the girl who had disappeared. She had also taken my good winter coat along with the cash from my wallet, around fifty bucks. I was less upset about the cash than I was about the coat. I had a spare, but it wasn't nearly as nice as the one she had taken. On the other hand, would I really have wanted her to leave my coat in the car? A pregnant woman who wasn't even wearing a sweater?

No, it was good she took my coat, no matter how irked I was about losing it. At least she hadn't taken my car.

I ended up not being able to leave until dark. The paramedics insisted on checking me out, even though I told them I hadn't actually been in the burning building. And then I had to repeat what happened to not just Max, but also to a cop who had arrived after the fire had more or less been extinguished. I had never met her before—she was middle-aged with salt and pepper hair that was pulled back in a messy ponytail and no makeup. With a no-nonsense approach, she asked me a bunch of questions and took just as many notes. I asked her if she was going to form a search party for the girl, because despite everything, I was still worried about her. After realizing she had disappeared, my initial reaction had been to go looking for her, but Max wouldn't let me leave. This surprised me. She was young and pregnant, after all, and had gone through a massively traumatic ordeal. I was sure she wasn't thinking straight. Someone needed to go after her.

The cop, though, seemed oddly … unconcerned. "We'll get one together," she said, but the lack of urgency was obvious. In fact, she even made a slight face as she spoke. "I'm sure she's fine. Probably went to a friend's house."

I stared at her. A friend's house? I was sure my expression was as perplexed as I felt. "How do you even know she lives around here?"

Now it was her turn to look perplexed. "If she worked here, she lived around here." Her voice was flat, and there was a finality to it … like she was done with the conversation.

I wasn't, though. I had a million questions. But when I opened my mouth to ask one, she immediately interrupted, asking me if there was anything else I wanted to share, and if not, I could go home. Of course, with the caveat that she might have more questions for me in the future.

"But what if I have questions?" I asked, but she was already turning away.

If I hadn't been so exhausted and cold, I might have pressed the issue, but as it was, I decided to drop it. I watched her walk over to her car and pick up the radio. Maybe she was calling in a search team for the girl after all. Just because she seemed a little put off when I asked about it didn't mean she wasn't going to do it. Maybe she was irritated because she thought I was trying to tell her how to do her job.

As unpleasant as the female cop was, I could at least be grateful that Officer Brandon Wyle wasn't the one to show up to question me. Just the thought made my stomach twist. I could just imagine his reaction. He would not be at all happy that I was even thinking about going into a burning building and surely would have treated me to his "let the professionals handle it" lecture.

And, while he had a point when it came to rescuing someone from a fire, if I hadn't been there—if I had decided to hunt down a phone rather than walk around the building—the girl likely wouldn't have made it out. Over and over in my head, I kept hearing the sound of the roof caving in. The firefighters had barely arrived on the scene when it happened. Maybe she would have been lucky and survived, but maybe not.

By the time I made it home, it was fully dark, and I was ready to drop from cold and exhaustion. I immediately went to the kitchen and got the kettle going for tea and threw some frozen homemade three-bean soup into a pot for dinner. Midnight, my black cat, was waiting impatiently in the kitchen, so I also fed him. While everything heated up, I called my tea clients to let them know something had come up, and I would drop off their orders the next day. I didn't give them specifics, as I was having enough trouble keeping myself focused on the task at hand. Again and again, I kept picturing the pregnant girl in my mind's eye, covered with soot and coughing as she wandered through the streets of Redemption in the dark and cold. At least she had my coat. And my fifty bucks, which wouldn't get her far, but it was something. Hopefully, the cop was right, and she did find her way to a friend's house. I just didn't have a good feeling about it. Something was off, but I couldn't put my finger on what, exactly. Just a niggling sensation that there was something more going on than just a building on fire.

A lot more.

Thankfully, my clients were also my friends, and they were all understanding about the delay. Maybe I would tell them the full story when I saw them.

After I ate, I took a long, hot shower, crawled into bed, and fell asleep almost immediately.

And dreamed.

It was a *raging* bonfire. So hot, my face felt like it was burning, and I could even smell the soot and ash. The orange-red flames were everywhere, licking at the walls, the ceiling. I could even see the dark shapes of trees, their bare branches reaching out, almost as if they were trying to trap me.

But that made no sense. Why would there be trees and a building?

The flames whipped around me, the crackling filling my ears and drowning everything else out. Actually, that wasn't true. I did hear something else. A voice. Low and monotonous. I couldn't make out the words, but it sounded almost like … a chant.

Or a curse.

I woke up with a start, gasping for breath and covered in sweat, even though my bedroom was cool and dark. Midnight was curled up next to me, snoring slightly.

I lay there for a few minutes, staring at the ceiling as I forced myself to take slow, deep breaths. *I'm fine*, I repeated to myself. *There is no fire. It's just a nightmare.*

And, quite honestly, was it that much of a surprise? To dream about being in a fire after the day I had? I pushed aside the little voice that reminded me how long it had been since I last had a nightmare in this house, and what it might mean if they were back. I shook my head and focused on untangling myself from the sheets. It was early, just after five, but I already knew there would be no more sleep.

Midnight woke up as I was pulling on my robe. He stretched, hopped off the bed, and padded toward the bedroom door. His emerald eyes glowed slightly as he looked back at me, tail flicking as he impatiently waited for me to get him his breakfast.

At least someone was happy I was up so early.

***

"Why didn't you call me?" Pat's voice on the other end of the line sounded hurt.

I cradled the phone between my shoulder and ear as I opened the oven to pull out a batch of zucchini muffins. Pat had been one of my first tea customers and ended up becoming one of my best friends. And while I normally would have called her if I had come upon a burning building in the middle of Redemption, it wasn't exactly a "normal" situation. I already knew she didn't approve of my going to that area of Redemption on a regular basis, and I had been so exhausted and worried about the pregnant girl, I just didn't want a lecture on either finding a different way to deliver tea to Hattie or getting rid of her altogether as a client.

But that didn't stop me from feeling a tinge of guilt.

"I was going to call you today," I said, even though I wasn't sure if that was completely true. "Last night, I was just so exhausted by the time I got home. But how did you find out what happened?"

"Charlie, are you kidding me?" She sounded exasperated. "You're on the front page of the paper."

"*What?*" Even I could hear the horror in my voice. "I'm on the front page? You mean by name?" Oh no. If that were the case, then everyone in town would already know what had happened.

Including Officer Brandon Wyle.

She let out a loud sigh. "Don't tell me you haven't gotten your paper yet."

I looked helplessly around my kitchen. "Well, I've been a little busy." Which was true. I had been baking nonstop since I'd gotten up, and my kitchen was full of fresh cookies, muffins, quick breads, and even a couple of bacon, egg, and cheese casseroles. I figured I could freeze them for later. I found baking soothing, and after looking at the amount I had baked, I apparently needed a lot of soothing.

"You've been baking, haven't you? Wait, don't answer that. I'll be right over." She didn't bother to say goodbye before simply hanging up.

I replaced the receiver, feeling more and more uneasy. I was on the front page of *The Redemption Times*? And no one at the paper had even called me for a quote? What had they printed about me? Did I even want to know?

On autopilot, I went to the coffeemaker to get a pot brewing. Pat loved tea, but in the morning, she loved coffee more. Plus, I had a feeling I was going to need some coffee myself.

Especially if ...

The phone rang again before I had even finished my thought. With trepidation, I picked up the receiver. "Hello?"

"Charlie, why didn't you call me last night?"

I closed my eyes. It was Wyle. The exact person I was afraid it was going to be. And he sounded really mad.

"I guess you saw the paper, as well."

"Paper? You mean the newspaper?" He sounded even more irate, which didn't seem possible. "You think I'm getting my information from the *newspaper*? No, I talked to Officer Capshaw."

"Oh," I said weakly. I assumed Officer Capshaw was the no-nonsense cop who interviewed me and thought it was too much to ask to search for a pregnant and traumatized girl, but I decided not to clarify. Wyle sounded upset enough. "Have you had breakfast?"

"What?" Now he sounded as if I had lost my mind.

"Breakfast. I have plenty of food here. Fresh baked muffins and a bacon and egg casserole. I just got the coffee started, and Pat is on her way."

"Why am I not surprised?" he grumbled. He paused for only a half-second before replying, "I'll be over in ten minutes."

I hung up the phone and sprinted up the stairs. While it wouldn't have bothered me to have Pat see me in my robe, with Wyle joining the party, I needed to at least get myself somewhat presentable.

***

"I can't believe you didn't call me," Pat grumbled a second time when I opened the front door. She was standing on my stoop, bundled up in an oversized gray winter jacket. In one matching gray-gloved hand, she held my newspaper, and in the other, a teacup poodle.

"And a good morning to you, too," I said as I gestured for her to come inside. "Coffee is just about ready."

Pat tried to glare at me, but I could already see her resolve melting. "Are those zucchini muffins I smell?"

"Freshly baked." Pat loved my zucchini muffins. Well, to be honest, she loved pretty much everything I baked.

I could see the struggle on her face. She still wanted to be miffed at me for not calling her, but the lure of baked goods was too strong. She sighed as she stepped inside, handing me my newspaper and her wriggling poodle before unwrapping herself.

"Hello Tiki," I said, greeting the excited little dog. Today, Tiki wore a dark-blue sweater with a teddy bear on the front of it and matching ribbons in her hair. She gave me a happy bark and licked my fingers. "Why yes, I did bake some doggy treats. How did you know?"

"You're going to spoil that dog," Pat muttered, but there was no heat behind it. She hung her jacket and scarf on the coatrack behind her, revealing her own matching dark-blue sweater, though it sported snowflakes rather than a teddy bear. Pat was a good decade or so older than me, and the best way to describe her was round: plump, with a round face, round black-rimmed glasses, and short, no-nonsense brown hair that was turning gray. She rubbed her hands together, blowing on them, before following me into the kitchen. Tiki had already beaten us both there and was busy greeting Midnight, who was curled up on his favorite chair next to the large window that overlooked the backyard. In the summer, it was a riot of color and green, as I had a massive garden that covered most of the yard. It was where I grew the herbs and flowers I used in my teas, but now, in the dead of winter, it was a desolate, lonely place blanketed with icy white snow and bare trees.

"You're not off the hook, you know," Pat said as she plucked a muffin from the platter I had displayed in the middle of the butcher-block table. "I still want to know why you didn't call me."

Before I could answer, the doorbell rang again. "You and Wyle both," I said.

She raised an eyebrow. "That's Wyle, then?"

I shrugged. "What can I say? He wanted breakfast too."

I left Pat in the kitchen, shaking her head as she munched on her muffin and rummaged around for a coffee cup. Midnight was nosing Tiki back, who was standing on her hind legs, tail wagging furiously. Those two didn't always get along, especially when they first met. But since then, they'd become fast friends.

I wiped my hands on my soft, worn jeans as I approached the door. I had enough time to pull on an emerald-green sweater that brought out the green in my hazel eyes and run a quick comb through my wild, brownish-blondish locks. I thought about adding a little makeup, then decided against it. Wyle and I were just friends. I didn't need to put on makeup when a friend was coming over. It wouldn't even occur to me to do so if it were just Pat.

But as I went to open the door, I found myself wishing I had at least put on some lip gloss.

"I can't believe you didn't call me," Wyle said, his dark eyes narrowing at me. Unlike Pat, whom I think was irritated (and maybe even a little hurt), Wyle was *mad*. Really, really mad. His thick, dark hair was mussed up, as if he had been angrily running his hands through it, and I could see a muscle twitch near his square-cut jawline. I pushed down the fizzle of energy that lit up my nerve endings anytime I was near him. *We are friends*, I reminded myself. *Only friends.*

"Neither can Pat," I said, opening the door wider. "So you might as well come in and have some coffee and a muffin while we talk about it."

Wyle's eyes narrowed, and he looked even angrier, if such a thing were possible. "And for, that matter, I can't believe you invited Pat as well." He stomped into the house, using a little more force than necessary to wipe his boots.

"You'll be relieved to know you weren't the only one I didn't call," I said as he peeled off his black coat, revealing a broad chest and slim build under his uniform.

Wyle opened his mouth to say something, or more likely, to keep yelling at me, but Tiki chose that moment to burst upon the scene, her toenails clicking on the hardwood floors and tail wagging furiously. She jumped up on Wyle's leg, barely making it past his ankle, and gave him an adoring look.

Wyle glared in response but reached down to pet her. "I guess the gang really is all here."

"You'll feel better when you get some coffee into you," I said as I headed back into the kitchen, Wyle and Tiki at my heels.

Pat was already sitting at the butcher-block table, which she had arranged with three settings. Platters of muffins and quick breads were also laid out, along with butter, cream, and sugar.

"That egg thingy in the oven looks like it's about done, but I didn't want to take it out," Pat said, cupping her mug between her hands before nodding toward one of the settings. "Nice to see you, Wyle. I've already poured your coffee."

Wyle still didn't look happy, but he nodded toward Pat as he sat in the chair she'd indicated. "Appreciate it. I guess it's good to know I wasn't the only one Charlie didn't call."

"No, you're not," Pat said, giving me a hard look. I ignored her and went to the oven to pull out the casserole. "Bribing us with food is only going to go so far," she continued.

I grabbed the potholders as I opened the oven. "Just give me a minute, and then, both of you can yell at me to your heart's content. Actually, before you do, I need one other thing."

"And what would that be?" Wyle asked, a dangerous edge to his voice.

I ignored that too, even though it made my stomach flip. "I need to know if there's an update on the pregnant girl."

Chapter 3

Pat's jaw dropped. "Pregnant girl? What pregnant girl?"

Now it was my turn for a jaw-drop. "You don't know about the pregnant girl? Wasn't it in the newspaper article?"

Wyle was rubbing his forehead, a pained expression on his face. "This is why you should have called me last night," he said, shooting me another hard look.

"I don't understand," I said, depositing the bacon, egg, and cheese casserole in the center of the table before taking my seat. "You don't want people to know about the pregnant girl? Why ever not?"

Wyle sighed before giving Pat a meaningful look. "She's an 1888er."

Just like that, Pat's entire expression shifted. Her eyes went wide before completely shuttering. It would have been comical if I had the faintest idea of what was going on. "Oh." She started busying herself with the casserole.

I stared at them, but neither would meet my gaze. Wyle was busy buttering a muffin as Pat heaped casserole onto her plate. "Oh, come on," I said impatiently. "Stop this. You have to tell me what's going on."

"Trust me, it's better if you don't know," Pat said darkly.

I wanted to roll my eyes. "Oh, for Pete's sake. Does this have anything to do with why you don't like me taking care of Hattie?"

Pat's head shot up. "Is that how you got involved? Because of an 1888er?" She shook the spatula at me, causing bits of egg to fly off. Tiki's ears perked up. "I told you she was bad news. You should have cut ties with her a long time ago."

I looked at her in exasperation. "An 1888er? What are you even talking about?"

Pat sat back in her chair, a frustrated look on her face. "I can't believe you got sucked into this. You don't understand what you're asking."

"No, I don't," I said, trying to keep my own frustration out of my voice but failing miserably. "Why is it such a big deal to tell me what's going on?"

"Because it's a curse to talk about," Pat spat out, the words flinging out of her like she could no longer keep them inside.

I froze. All at once, my nightmare seemed to swamp me. I could practically feel the heat of the flames and smell the acrid smoke burning my nostrils.

And of course, the voice. The chanting. Even though I couldn't make out the words, I was sure it was a curse.

Pat was studying me, her expression unreadable, but there was a strange knowing in her eyes. "But you already know," she said, her voice quiet.

With some effort, I pushed the nightmare fragments aside. "I have no idea what you're talking about. What curse? And what is an 1888er?"

Wyle cleared his throat. "So, look. I'm fairly new here myself, but I'll tell you what I know. You know Redemption's history, right?"

I gave him a puzzled look. "You mean when all the adults disappeared?"

Wyle nodded slowly, his eyes sharpening. "Exactly. Do you remember the year it happened?"

What a strange question. Who cared when it happened? It was ancient history, and besides, what could it possibly have to do with a fire and a missing pregnant girl? "Yes, it was like 1880-something." My voice caught in my throat as the pieces started to fall into place, and my mouth went dry.

Wyle continued to hold my gaze. "1888."

Silence. The only sound was Tiki's snuffling as she nosed the table in search of the scattered eggs.

Redemption, Wisconsin definitely had a troubling, haunted past. Back in 1888, all the adults disappeared, leaving only the children.

No one knew what happened to them—the children all swore they knew nothing. They woke up one morning, and the adults were gone.

Since then, the town has had a history of strange and unexplained occurrences. Missing people. Ghosts. Hauntings. While it was true that there were more disappearances (and murders, for that matter) than there should be for a town the size of Redemption, it didn't necessarily mean the town itself was haunted. Or that the town somehow decided who lived here and who didn't, which was another old wives' tale connected to Redemption.

It was just rumors and stories. Fiction. That was it.

"So the 1888ers …" I started to say.

"Are direct descendants of the adults who disappeared," Wyle said.

My eyes widened. "Seriously? They know this?"

Wyle shrugged. "Apparently so."

"And they have an actual name for themselves?" This seemed so weird to me. "Is this like a club or something?"

Pat let out a bark of laughter that had no humor in it. "A club no one would ever want to join." She was holding her fork, but it didn't seem like she was eating. Rather, she seemed to be simply shuffling food around her plate, which was very unlike her. "You guys aren't going to drop this, are you?" She eyed both of us before letting out a loud sigh. "Fine." She put her fork down and reached for her coffee cup. Tiki gave her a little lick, as if for courage.

While I appreciated Pat's use of "you guys" rather than focusing specifically on me (which I was pretty sure was what she meant, as I was the one pushing it with Wyle), watching her was making me feel more than a little uneasy. Pat was usually happy to fill me in on whatever Redemption lore I was missing. The fact that she was so reluctant to do so in this situation was a little unnerving.

"While nobody knows what happened to the adults back in 1888, most people believe they were at least somewhat to blame. Either they did something naughty and paid the ultimate price for it, or they got caught up in something that ended badly for them."

"What do you mean, got caught up in something?" I asked.

Pat shrugged. "There are a lot of rumors, but one of the more popular ones is that they ended up on the wrong side of a fight with a band of Great Lakes pirates."

"Wait, there were pirates on the Great Lakes?" I asked.

"Back then, there were pirates everywhere," Wyle said.

"Yes, but a band of pirates?" I couldn't wrap my head around pirates from Lake Michigan being the cause of the adults disappearing.

Pat gave me a look. "Do you want me to continue or not?"

"I do," I said hastily. "Of course I do. I just never heard that explanation before. Or that they may have done something wrong."

"There has to be a reason for the adults being targeted but not the children," Pat said. "If it had been something natural—say a disease or a storm, or fire—every single adult likely wouldn't have disappeared, and some children would have been affected. But that's not what happened. So, if it wasn't natural, then it had to be deliberate. Hence, people believe the adults either did or didn't do something to cause it."

I reached out to take a muffin. "I guess when you say it like that, it seems obvious."

Pat shot me that look again that made it seem like she was trying very hard not to roll her eyes. "Regardless, it's not a huge leap, then, to say that the reason the adults disappeared was because they were cursed. And if the adults were cursed, then it's also not a huge leap to assume the curse extends to their bloodline. Which is what the 1888ers believe."

Again, my mind flashed back to my dream and the terrible chant that emerged from the flames. It had definitely sounded like a curse. "Let me get this straight," I said slowly, trying to push the images from my dream away. *It was just a coincidence*, I kept telling myself. *I stood next to a burning building earlier that day … of course I might dream about it.* "People believe the reason the adults disappeared back in 1888 was that they were cursed. And they were cursed because of something they did or didn't do. And that curse extended through their individual bloodlines, and now these … 1888ers, because they are direct descendants of the adults who disappeared, also believe they are cursed?"

"Exactly," Pat said.

Something in her tone made me shiver, and I reached for my coffee, wanting to at least hold it for warmth. "That's a depressing way to live. What about the whole 'the sins of the father should not be visited on the child' thing?"

"Apparently, at least according to the 1888ers, that doesn't apply to them," Pat said flatly.

As convinced as Pat was that curses existed, I wasn't so sure. There were so many holes in the story, I didn't even know where to start. "Yes, but … I didn't think pirates cursed people."

"It depends," Wyle said. "It's rumored that if you steal gold or treasure from certain pirates, you'll be cursed. Kind of like all the stories around stealing gold from an Egyptian tomb."

"So you think the adults in Redemption, Wisconsin, stole from a pirate … and that's why they were cursed?" The whole thing was sounding more and more fanciful. "How would that even work? It's not like we're that close to Lake Michigan."

"It's more likely than them raiding an Egyptian tomb," Wyle said.

"Well, yeah …" I started, but Pat interrupted.

"It doesn't matter what happened," she said, her voice sharp and face flustered. "All that matters is that there is a curse."

"Actually, I would say it does matter what the curse is," I said. "Not that I necessarily believe in curses, but if I did, you would need to know where the curse originated from to actually break it …"

Pat slammed her hand down on the table, causing everything to rattle and Tiki to jump. Coffee sloshed out of Wyle's cup, but otherwise, nothing broke. "You're not listening. You can't break this curse. All you can do is make sure you don't get caught up in it. Why do you think I keep telling you to stay away from the 1888ers? You need to leave it alone. Don't talk about them, don't spend time with them. Just leave them be."

I could feel my jaw drop. I had never seen Pat like that before. Her eyes were wild and her face was flushed. There were two red spots high on her cheekbones. "Pat, you must know there's no such thing as curses …"

She shook her head angrily. "No, just …" she paused, squeezed her eyes tightly shut, and took a few deep breaths, as if trying to get herself under control. "Look, I get it. You didn't grow up here. You didn't see what we, those of us who have been here for years, have seen." She opened her eyes and looked between Wyle and me. "If you had, you would understand. How the 1888ers are never able to get ahead, no matter what they do. You've seen that area of town where they live—how broken down and failing everything is. But that's just the beginning. All of them suffer enormous tragedies throughout their lives, whether it's their health or finances or both. And don't get me started on the children. Most of them have a lot of trouble having babies of their own. They either can't get pregnant, or they're plagued with miscarriages or stillbirths. And even if they do have a child, they're usually not healthy or end up in terrible accidents. It seems obvious that the 1888ers are slowly dying out. Their family lines are drying up. It's not happening all at once, but more like a slow drip … almost as if whatever cursed them is trying to extend the pain as long as possible. Trust me, you don't want anything to do with them. And luckily for us, they don't want anything to do with us either. They're happy to stay isolated in their small, dying community, and we should be thankful and leave it that way." She picked up her fork and scooped a bite of the egg casserole as Wyle and I stared at her.

Or, at least, I stared at her. I was pretty sure my jaw had fallen open, as well, and I could think of nothing to say. I had never seen this side of Pat before. Even if she didn't like someone, she wasn't harsh on them. But this was something else.

"Don't hold back, Pat. Tell us what you really think," Wyle said, and that seemed to break the tension. I let out a snicker, and even Pat half-smiled as she continued eating the casserole.

"Just you wait," Pat said, mouth full of egg, cheese, and bacon. "Someday, you'll thank me."

"I have no doubt," Wyle said mildly. "To be fair," he said to me with a meaningful look, "Pat is giving you good advice. It's better to leave the investigating to the professionals."

"Are the 'professionals' actually investigating?" I asked, putting air quotes around the word "professionals."

Wyle looked perplexed. "Why wouldn't they be?"

"I don't know, but the officer who was there yesterday didn't seem to be all that motivated to find a missing and possibly injured pregnant girl," I said.

"What part of not getting involved don't you understand?" Pat asked.

I lifted my hands in exasperation. "I heard you. The 1888ers are cursed. But there's still a pregnant girl wandering around out there who really needs medical attention. Someone needs to be looking out for her."

"We'll do what we can, but if she's an 1888er and doesn't want to be found, there isn't a lot we can do," Wyle said.

"Well, you should at least try," I said. "She was trapped in a burning building. And what about Arthur? Did you find him?"

"Arthur?" Pat asked, probably despite herself.

"The girl told me he was still in the building somewhere," I said. "For that matter, what kind of building was it? All I saw was a sign that read '88 Spir.'"

"Spir?" Pat asked, her brows knitting in confusion. "What's spir?"

"I have no idea," I said. "The rest of the letters were burned off."

"You don't mean 88 Spirits, do you?" Pat asked.

"I don't know, maybe," I said as Wyle pinched the bridge of his nose.

"If you aren't planning on investigating, it doesn't make sense to get into the details," Wyle said.

"What details?" I asked flabbergasted. "You mean the name of the business wasn't in the paper either?"

"It's a small town," Wyle said. "We're trying to keep things contained for as long as we possibly can."

I stared at him. "What does that even mean? What is going on here? Why is there so much secrecy around a fire?"

Wyle gave me a pained look before opening his mouth to answer, but the doorbell ringing interrupted him.

His expression instantly shifted to what I called his cop mask, his features smoothing out so it was impossible to read his face. "Are you expecting anyone?"

I stood up. "No. I guess I'd better see who it is."

Chapter 4

I briefly entertained the idea that it might be the pregnant girl, although that seemed unlikely. I was on the other side of town from her, and she didn't have any transportation, unless she used the cash she had found in my car on a cab. But that seemed silly. Why would she have run away in the first place if she was going to chase me down later? And how would she know where I lived … unless she memorized the address on my driver's license when she took my money.

Ugh.

But it wasn't the pregnant girl.

"Good morning," Tilde Tillerson said with a big grin and a pointed look in her eyes. Her brittle orange hair flew around her head like a dandelion fluff, somehow matching the orange frames of her glasses. However, both clashed with her bright-red jacket and violet scarf. "How was your day yesterday?"

"Um," I said, blinking at her.

"I just came by to pick up my tea order," Mildred Schmidt, who was standing next to Tilde, said. She had folded her arms across her chest, and even though her long, black winter coat looked warm, she was still shivering. "I don't suppose you could let us in?" She asked, stamping her feet.

"And maybe invite us to have a cup of coffee while you're at it?" Tilde asked. "I missed my morning cup."

"And maybe a cookie?" Mildred asked.

Tilde elbowed her. "It's too early for cookies. Maybe a muffin."

They both stared hopefully at me, and I could see the glint in their eyes.

They had come to pump me for details about the fire.

I sighed, picturing Wyle's chagrin, but I had a feeling if I turned them down, they would find another way to get into the house.

Maybe Tilde would fake a heart attack, or Mildred would simply break into my garage.

"Come on in," I said, holding the door wider. "I hope you're hungry. I've got plenty of food."

Both of their faces brightened noticeably, although whether from the offer of food or the possibility of gathering information, I wasn't sure.

Tilde and Mildred were both tea clients and the owners of The Redemption Detective Agency, along with Tilde's niece Emily and a bookstore owner named Nora. Well, on second thought, Tilde was an owner for sure. I was less sure about the other's involvement. All I really knew about it was that Pat thought it was a colossal waste of time. Tilde was a retired nurse; Mildred was a retired teacher; Nora was a business owner in the same strip mall that the agency was located, and Emily was a former COO. So it wasn't like any of them knew anything about being a private detective.

Nevertheless, what they lacked in training and experience, they made up for in enthusiasm—hence why there were on my porch bright and early.

"Who is it?" Pat called out.

Tilde looked up in delight. "Oh good, Pat is here. Hello," she sang out. "It's Tilde and Mildred."

There were a couple of thuds and some muttering (I was unclear who was doing it), and then Pat's voice sounded again. "I'll make another pot of coffee."

"Good idea," I called out, wrinkling my nose as Mildred removed her winter coat and I got a strong whiff of her floral perfume. Her gray hair looked freshly set, and her bright-red lipstick matched her red turtleneck, red and black sweater, and black trousers. This was in stark contrast to Tilde's purple sweater covered with pink and yellow flowers (I wondered briefly where Tilde could have even found a sweater like that) paired with a turtleneck that was a completely different shade of purple than the sweater and bright-blue pants.

Tilde finished removing her boots and straightened up, rubbing her hands together. "It smells wonderful, Charlie."

"Well, there's plenty, so help yourselves," I said as I led them into the kitchen. Pat was still bustling around the coffee pot while Wyle remained sitting at the table with a very unhappy expression on his face.

"Wyle, I didn't realize you were here," Tilde said as she sat herself.

Wyle swallowed a mouthful of food before giving both of them a rather pained smile. "Tilde, Mildred."

"So you must be here about the fire, too," Mildred said, sitting next to Tilde and reaching for a muffin.

Wyle held up his coffee cup. "I'm just here for breakfast."

"Oh nonsense," Tilde said, rolling her eyes. "Of course that's why you're here. You probably want Charlie's help finding out who killed Arthur."

Wyle's hand jerked, sloshing coffee over his mug and onto his hand, before he quickly lowered it. "How do you know about Arthur?"

"He's the owner of 88 Spirits, isn't he?" Mildred asked as she started buttering a muffin.

"Wait, how did you know it was 88 Spirits that burned?" Pat asked as she brought over the full coffeepot to fill mugs. Wyle closed his eyes and pinched his nose again. "It wasn't in the paper."

"What, you think that's the only place we get our news?" Tilde waved her hand. "I've got eyes and ears all over town."

Somehow, I didn't doubt that.

"I had Arthur as a student," Mildred remarked as she started doctoring her coffee with cream and sugar. "I have to say, I'm not entirely surprised he found himself in a spot of trouble."

A spot of trouble? Every nerve ending in my body was tingling, but before I could ask more, Wyle jumped in.

"Wait, why were you teaching Arthur?" Wyle asked. "Wasn't he an 1888er?"

Mildred looked at him in confusion. "Why wouldn't I have 1888ers as students? It's not like they had a school in that dreadful little area they live in. If they don't want to or can't be homeschooled, there aren't a lot of options."

"I didn't think they left that area of town," I said.

"They will if they need to," Tilde said. "I've had 1888ers as patients. If they need medical attention, where else are they going to go? Sure, they mostly keep to themselves, but there are times they have no choice but to leave. And not all of the 1888ers are committed to living separately. Some of them have even told me they wished they lived somewhere else."

"Well, of course they do," Pat said. "They're cursed. Why wouldn't they want to try to get away from it? Never mind that they might end up inadvertently passing it to someone else."

"I don't think curses are catching," Tilde said. "Although I agree they do have a lot of bad luck. It's really quite sad."

"You can't catch their curse," Mildred said firmly, as if she were an expert in all things curses. "It's like a blood disease. You either have it, or you don't."

"How do you know how curses work?" Pat snapped. I was actually wondering the same thing. "Curses very well could be catching. I, for one, have no desire to take a chance on it."

The conversation was going nowhere. Besides, I was still stuck on what Mildred had said earlier. "So, back to Arthur," I said, leaning forward. "What spot of trouble was he in?"

"Can't we just enjoy breakfast?" Wyle asked, but I could see that despite himself, his interest was piqued as well.

"What's wrong with you?" I asked him. "Why don't you want anyone to know about these fires?"

Wyle's eyes shifted toward me as they narrowed. "There's nothing wrong with me. I just wanted to enjoy a nice breakfast and not talk shop." Even though he said the words in a neutral tone, I could hear the lie underneath.

"Then why are you wearing your uniform?" Tilde asked.

Wyle started. "I'm … I'm working later." Now, he really did sound as if he were lying. "But obviously, I'm overruled, so Mildred, why don't you tell us what you mean?"

Mildred gave him a look like she wasn't buying anything he said either, but just because she didn't believe him wasn't going to stop her from taking the spotlight. "He was always a magnet for the girls. Even as a child. It was clear even then that he was going to have trouble staying celibate. So, the fact that he knocked up one of his waitresses …"

"*What?*" I let out something of a screech as my hand jerked, spilling hot coffee all over it. "Ouch!"

Tilde's eyes went wide as she jumped out of her chair. "Oh no. Charlie, are you okay? Let me get a washcloth."

"I'm fine. Just get one out of the sink to wipe up the table, please," I said as I set the mug down, shaking my hand. "I mostly just scared myself. Are you saying the pregnant girl was Arthur's mistress?" I pictured the girl again, so young and scared. "How old is Arthur anyway?"

Mildred frowned. "Oh, I'd have to check my records, but I'm sure he must be in his late thirties or early forties."

My eyes went wide. "In his forties?"

"How do you know Edie?" Tilde asked as she handed me the washcloth.

"Edie? That's the name of the pregnant girl?" How was it that everyone else knew what was going on before I did?

"If you're talking about a waitress at 88 Spirits who was also pregnant, that's probably Edie," Tilde said. "I doubt every pregnant girl out there is named Edie."

"Why do you keep calling her a girl?" Pat asked, her eyes steady on me.

"Because she's young," I said.

"How young?" Pat asked.

"Well, I didn't look at her driver's license, if that's what you're asking, but she couldn't have been any older than early twenties," I said. "Maybe even late teens."

Tilde put her hand to her chest. "Oh my goodness. That's practically illegal."

Mildred shook her head. "I'm not surprised. He always was a bit of a scoundrel."

I was only half-listening to them. Instead, I was near that burning building again, with Edie telling me that Arthur was still in the bar, but it wasn't safe for me to go after him. "I wonder why she was alone."

"What do you mean?" Pat asked.

"Well, Edie, if that's who it was," I said slowly, trying to piece it together. "She was on the ground floor. But Arthur was somewhere else."

"How do you know that?" Pat asked.

"Because Edie told me Arthur was trapped somewhere, but I shouldn't go in after him because the roof was going to cave," I said. "But why was she the only person there? Where was everyone else?"

"The bar probably hadn't opened yet, and they were … well, you know," Mildred said meaningfully.

Ugh. While I had no idea what Arthur looked like, I definitely didn't want that image in my head. "If that were the case, why wasn't Arthur with her? Why was he somewhere else where he couldn't get out?"

"Maybe he was trying to find another way out," Pat said. "You said Edie was trapped in there, right?"

"Right," I said doubtfully. "But why wouldn't they go together to find another way out?"

"You said he was trapped. Maybe he couldn't free her," Pat said. "He thought it would be faster to find a way out and call for help."

I shook my head. "She wasn't trapped like that. The back door was blocked."

"Blocked?" Wyle had straightened ever so slightly, and his gaze bored into mine. "How was it blocked?"

"There was a block of wood wedged in front of it," I explained. "There was no way she could open it from the inside."

"The door was actually blocked?" Tilde asked, her eyes widening as she stared at me. Actually, Pat and Mildred were also staring at me with the same expressions on their faces. "Are you saying someone trapped her inside?"

"It was probably Arthur they were trying to trap," Mildred said. "Maybe his wife did it because he was cheating on her."

Arthur was married? I opened my mouth to ask, but Pat spoke first. "Wait a minute. You're saying the fire was deliberate? And that they were also trying to kill someone?"

"I'm sure that's not what happened," Wyle said quickly. A little too quickly. "It's entirely possible the fire loosened some boards that just fell on the door in such a way that they kept it from opening."

He sounded so sure of himself. Yet when I pictured the door and how the piece of wood was wedged under it, it didn't seem accidental to me. "But it was really wedged under there."

"If either Edie or Arthur tried to get out, and the wood was positioned just right, it's possible they were the ones who jammed it, albeit accidentally," Wyle said.

"That seems far-fetched," I said, picturing Edie standing by the back window, begging for help. She was the one who told me the door was blocked, which means either she or Arthur had tried to open it and couldn't.

Wyle gave me a look. "More far-fetched than someone trying to block the door so they couldn't get out?"

"Why is that far-fetched?" I asked. "I would think if you wanted to kill someone, trapping them in a burning building would be an effective way to do it. Along with getting rid of the person, it would also get rid of a lot of the evidence. Right?"

"But it's not an effective way to kill someone, as evidenced by what happened with Edie," Wyle said. "If this was attempted murder, they did a terrible job, because she was able to escape."

"Just because someone wants to kill someone doesn't mean they're going to be good at it," I said. "As evidenced by what happened with Edie."

Wyle made a face at me. "We're also jumping to conclusions. We don't know if this was attempted murder or not."

"But the door ..." I started to say, but Wyle interrupted me.

"We don't know if the door was actually blocked or not," Wyle said. "Like I said, it could have been just dumb luck that a piece of wood fell in just the right spot."

Again, I pictured the blocked door in my head. It didn't feel like it was just a big coincidence. But Wyle was right; how could I prove it?

"So was Arthur killed or not?" Tilde asked.

"It's still early in the investigation," Wyle said. "We don't know anything."

"But there was a body?" I asked.

Wyle gave me a pained look. "Yes, but we still need to identify it, as well as determine how the fire started. It could have been an accident …"

"It's Arthur," Mildred said decisively. "I'm sure of it. Mark my words. His wife is behind the whole thing, because she wanted to get rid of the embarrassment of her husband and his employee-lover having a baby together."

That actually sounded more plausible than I wanted to admit.

"Let's not jump to conclusions," Wyle said. "As I said, we don't even know if the fire was deliberate."

"And even if it were, we shouldn't get involved," Pat said. "Especially if it was his wife. Let the 1888ers take care of their own, is what I say."

"Okay, so that's probably not going to happen either," Wyle said. "The police will investigate, as they should …"

Pat, Mildred, and Tilde all burst into laughter, interrupting Wyle and leaving us both staring at them in befuddlement.

"I don't understand why that's funny," Wyle said. "If we find proof of foul play, of course we'll investigate."

"Yeah, you'll investigate alright," Mildred said. "You'll investigate it right into the Redemption Police Department's basement."

Wyle looked almost offended. "If there was a murder, or an attempted murder, or both, it absolutely will not end up in the department's basement." But despite his words, his voice held a note of unease.

Tilde wiped her eyes and leaned over to squeeze his hand. "You're a good cop, Wyle. But you'll learn soon enough. When you do, it's important to keep one thing in mind."

Wyle gave her a wary look. "What's that?"

"It's not your fault."

Chapter 5

I had just finished wiping the counters and was about to make a pot of tea when the doorbell rang.

I paused, tea in one hand, trying to imagine who it could possibly be. Wyle, Pat, Tilde, and Mildred had left a couple of hours before. I had just finished cleaning up the kitchen, so I couldn't imagine it was any of them.

Unless … could it possibly be Edie?

No, I was sure it wasn't, for the same reasons I thought earlier. It made no sense for Edie to duck out of my car and run off only to come out of hiding and find me the very next day.

But this time, I wasn't sure how I felt about it.

The morning had ended on a bit of a sour note. Wyle had ended up in an argument with Pat, Mildred, and Tilde, during which he defended the Redemption police force. The three ladies … well, they had been pretty condescending, all things considered. Wyle had finally left in a huff, which I didn't blame him for, but I had to hurry after him to catch him before he disappeared.

"What, Charlie?" he grumbled as he shoved his arms through the sleeves of his winter coat.

Oh boy. I was hoping to sweet-talk some information out of him, which would have been easier to do if he wasn't already in a foul mood. I stepped closer to him. "I was just curious … why is this fire so hush-hush? Apparently, the paper didn't even publish the name of the building that burned. Why the secrecy?"

He didn't answer immediately, instead zipping up his jacket and pulling on his gloves. "For the same reason we always try to limit information provided to the media," he finally said. "So it's easier for us to determine who actually knows something from all the crackpots."

"Yes, but the name of the building?" I pressed. "Surely that's hardly a secret. Anyone who drives by would see it."

He gave me a sideways look. "Who is going to drive by? You were there. It's at the end of a dead-end road."

Well, that was true. "Yes, but ..."

"Charlie, just leave it," he snapped. So much for me trying to bribe him with food. "This is complicated enough without giving away all the details."

I stepped back, feeling a little stung. "Fair enough, but then why was I named in the paper?"

He gave me another sideways look. "You tell me."

"What?" I didn't know what he was talking about.

"You're the one with a past," he said, his eyes narrowing. "Yes, it would have been better if your name wasn't in there, but there's only so much we can do."

My jaw dropped. "What does that mean?"

Wyle pressed his lips together, as if he had said too much. "I need to go. But listen to Pat and let the professionals handle this, okay?" He didn't wait for me to answer, instead wrenching the front door open. "And, yes, we WILL handle it." His voice was grim as he stomped off into the bitter cold.

I shut the door behind him, my mind racing. What was Wyle talking about? Maybe I'd better see for myself what was in the paper.

I headed back to the kitchen just in time to see Pat, Mildred, and Tilde getting ready to leave. Mildred and Tilde had to get back to the agency, and Pat had some errands to run before she was due at one of the many volunteer jobs she was constantly juggling.

"Charlie, promise me you'll stay away from this case," Pat said. "Let Wyle handle it."

"You guys just spent the past fifteen minutes insisting that the police department wasn't going to handle it."

"Well, yeah," Pat said, not meeting my eyes. "But that doesn't mean you should get involved, either. Just let it be. It will be handled."

"By whom?" I asked. "If not me and not the police department, who is going to look into it?"

"Someone will," Tilde said.

I gave her a hard look. "You mean like the Redemption Detective Agency?"

Her eyes went wide. "Oh, heaven's no. We're not going to have anything to do with it."

"And not because of any curse," Mildred added, giving Pat a sideways glance. Pat made a face back at her.

"But why not?" I asked. It felt like pulling teeth. Why was it so difficult to get a straight answer in this case?

Tilde patted my arm. "There are some things in Redemption that are just better to leave alone. Trust us. Everything will work out fine."

All three of them paused and stared pointedly at me. As much as I wanted to keep asking questions, there was something about the way they were all hyper-focused on me that was making me uneasy.

"Okay," I said, and all of them immediately relaxed as they let out long breaths, as if they had been holding them while they waited for my answer.

This was just getting stranger and stranger.

As soon as they left, I unrolled the newspaper. I had expected the story to be the first one, as Pat had told me it was on the front page. But it was actually a tiny, three-paragraph article on the bottom right with the headline *Ramshackle Building Burned.*

Ramshackle? This was a business they were referring to, not some derelict house about to collapse.

I quickly skimmed the story, which didn't say much other than one of Redemption's older, not very well-maintained buildings had burned down, and police were currently investigating the cause.

I was mentioned in the third paragraph.

When the police and fire departments arrived, they only found one person, Charlie Kingsley, a local tea maker and owner of Helen Blackstone's house, which she had purchased a few years back. According to the police, she had seen the fire and stopped to offer assistance.

What on Earth?

How was it that there was more about me in this article than the bar that had burned down? Or the person who may have died in the fire? Or the second person, who was pregnant and now missing after escaping the blaze?

Either this was an example of truly shoddy journalism … or the paper was so desperate to cover *something* other than the actual fire that they decided to make it all about me. Neither explanation was reassuring.

It made me wonder if Tad was somehow involved. He was a journalist at *The Redemption Times*, and we had clashed more than once. Was that the reason why the paper had chosen to focus on me? Was that what Wyle meant?

Ugh. So frustrating. All I had were questions and no clear way to get any answers.

I crumpled up the paper and threw myself into cleaning the kitchen. That, at least, I could control. And maybe Pat and company were right, and I just needed to leave it. No one else seemed to want to investigate this case. Maybe I should follow suit. It wasn't like I didn't have enough other things to do. I had to finish making all the deliveries I was supposed to make yesterday, along with buying a new winter coat.

I had just about convinced myself of that when the doorbell rang. And just like that, I was back to wondering if Edie was on the other side of the door.

Get a hold of yourself, Charlie, I muttered to myself as I went to answer it. It was more likely that it was one of my tea clients who decided to stop by and pick up her order since I was taking too long to deliver it.

But it wasn't a tea client. In fact, it wasn't anyone I knew.

"Are you Charlie Kingsley?" The woman standing on my front stoop wore an expensive-looking red and black ski jacket with a matching red hat, scarf, and gloves. Her oversized sunglasses hid much of her face, which seemed a little overkill for the Wisconsin sun that continuously disappeared behind the clouds, and her knitted beanie hat with a white pompom was pulled low over her forehead.

"I am," I said cautiously. While I was fairly certain that I had never met this woman, it was difficult to tell with so much fabric covering her face.

"I know you don't know me, but I was hoping I could have a few minutes of your time," she said.

"Would you mind telling me what this is about?" I asked, shifting from one foot to the other as I tried to keep the door as closed as possible. I wasn't loving standing in the doorway and letting all the heat out, but I also wasn't going to invite this woman in until I had some idea who she was and what she wanted.

Her mouth, which was painted with red lipstick that also matched the ensemble, twisted into something resembling a smile. "Fair enough. I'm Carol Mueller. My husband owned 88 Spirits."

I blanched. "Your husband was Arthur?"

She slowly nodded.

I stepped back and held the door open wider. "Come in." I was amazed to find her on my doorstep. It hadn't even been 24 hours since the fire, and she had managed to pull herself together to come to my house? I couldn't imagine what she could possibly want.

She stepped inside, stomping her Moon boots on the welcome mat before removing all her winter layers and hanging them up on the coat rack next to the door. "I was just about to make myself a pot of tea. Would you like some?"

"Tea sounds lovely," she said. She hadn't removed her sunglasses yet, but I could now see her hair, which was expensively cut in a short, stylish bob with blonde highlights. Her sweater was a soft, camel-colored cashmere. Her purse was a Chanel, and I caught a whiff of what smelled like Chanel perfume.

I thought about what Pat had said about the 1888ers not having much luck or success with much of anything, but based solely on what Carol was wearing, she certainly didn't seem to have any financial problems. Unless, of course, she was living on credit cards and debt.

I led her into the kitchen, where I waved her to the table while I finished making tea. I also gathered a few leftover muffins and put them on a plate. She thanked me when I put everything out but didn't make a move toward the food. Instead, she cupped her tea between her hands. I noticed her nails were beautifully manicured and painted a pale pink. She still hadn't removed her sunglasses. While the sun's reflection on the white snow mixed with the cheery yellow and white color scheme of my kitchen did make the room bright, wearing sunglasses seemed a bit much.

"Do you need me to pull down the shades?" I gestured toward the window.

She started. "Oh." She reached up and patted her sunglasses. "No, no, that's fine." She removed them, and I could immediately see why she hadn't taken them off. Her eyes were puffy and bloodshot, probably from crying, and I instantly felt a twist of guilt that I had said anything at all. Of course she would be crying, and obviously, she was trying to hide it.

"It's been tough," she said quietly as she folded them up and carefully placed them next to her tea. "As I'm sure you can imagine."

"I'm so sorry for your loss," I said as I slid into the seat across from her. "So I take it that ..."

"It's not confirmed yet," she said, staring down into her tea. She had gone back to holding it between her hands. "There was a body found in 88 Spirits, but it's ... his ..." she swallowed hard. "The body was badly burned, so we're waiting for identification. Dental records. Hopefully, it will happen today or tomorrow." She lifted her head and gazed out at the winter wonderland. "But I'm sure it's him." Her voice was soft.

"I'm really sorry," I said again.

She didn't say anything for a moment, just stared outside as if lost in memories before giving herself a quick shake. "Thank you. And it's why I'm here."

"How can I help you?" I asked, although inwardly, I was already bracing myself. Was she going to ask me to tell her what happened yesterday? How I had rescued that pregnant girl who might have been Arthur's lover? Oh man, I really didn't want to do that. Not to mention, what would Wyle say? Mildred's voice kept running through my mind, as well ... how she was convinced Arthur's wife had something to do with the fire. Was that why she was here? To pick my brain, so she could plan her story?

Wyle was going to strangle me if I ruined his case. For that matter, I might strangle myself if I ruined the case. I was going to have to tread carefully.

But her answer surprised me. "You're Charlie Kingsley, the detective, right?"

I could feel my brow furrow. "Um … I am Charlie Kingsley, but I make and sell custom teas. I'm not a detective."

She rolled her eyes as she waved her hand. "I know you're not an actual detective, like with the police. But you're … what do they call it? When you don't get paid for doing something?"

"Like a hobby?"

"Yes, like a hobby. You solve mysteries as a hobby, right?"

"Um … yes, I guess so." Wyle was really going to have my head.

While it was true that I had solved a handful of cases, more or less, since I moved to Redemption, it wasn't anything I looked for. I made and sold custom teas, and I would have been perfectly content if that was all I did.

But, for better or for worse, my tea clients seemed to have a knack for finding themselves in trouble with the law. Luckily for them, I had a knack for solving mysteries and getting them out of trouble with the law. However, I never thought of myself as a detective, amateur or otherwise. More like a helpful friend.

Carol closed her eyes briefly at my answer. "Oh, thank goodness," she breathed before opening her eyes. Her expression shifted, and she leaned forward, her eyes intense. "I need your help. I need you to find who killed my husband and set fire to our bar."

46

Chapter 6

I blinked, momentarily taken aback by her reaction. While I was usually more than happy to jump in and help anyone out if they found themselves caught up in a murder investigation, in this case, I wasn't so sure. Pat's warnings kept lingering in my head, and I also couldn't shake the fact that I didn't know Carol. At all.

How would I know if she had had anything to do with her husband's death or not?

"Don't you think the police are better suited for that?" I asked, mostly to try to stall for time.

Her expression darkened. "The police," she spat. "They're not going to do anything."

Again, I pictured the scene from earlier, with Pat, Mildred, and Tilde laughing as Wyle got more and more frustrated. What was going on? What did basically everyone else in Redemption seem to know that I, and presumably Wyle, didn't? "But if it's a murder investigation, surely …"

"It's the 1888ers." Her voice was flat, almost dismissive.

I waited a beat, expecting her to say more, but she just stared at me, as if what she had given me was a complete answer.

I took a deep breath. "Look, you'll have to forgive me, but I actually have no idea what you're talking about. Why would the police not care about a murder investigation just because the 1888ers are involved? They care about other murders in Redemption."

Her expression was unreadable as she continued to study me. "You didn't grow up in Redemption, did you?"

I let out a small laugh. "I didn't even grow up in Wisconsin, much less Redemption. I moved here a few years ago from New York."

She sank back in her chair, nodding her head. "Oh, of course. I think I did know that, but I …" she waved her hand. "It slipped my mind. Sorry."

"There's nothing for you to apologize for. You've had a terrible time, and I'm not surprised you don't remember."

A ghost of a smile touched her lips, but it didn't reach her eyes. "I'm assuming you know the town's history."

"That all the adults disappeared in 1888? Yes, and I also know that the 1888ers are descendants of the adults who disappeared."

"So then you know that the 1888ers are cursed."

"Well … um … yes, I guess that's true." I almost said I didn't believe in curses until I realized she wasn't asking me about my beliefs.

She must have seen the skepticism on my face, though, because she gave me an exasperated look. "They ARE cursed, you know."

I wasn't going to argue with a woman who had just lost her husband. "Okay," I started to say as realization sank in. "Wait a minute. Aren't you an 1888er?"

She looked as if she were about to roll her eyes again. "Do I look like one?" She gestured to her expensive clothes, her lovely nails.

"Um …" What was I supposed to say to that? I felt like I was about to insult her. "I guess I did hear that the 1888ers were, um, not terribly successful."

"You can say it. They're failures." Her voice was bitter. "None of them have any money. Or a lot of luck, at least the good kind. And my goodness, if you let them, they'll tell you all about how it's impossible for any of them to get ahead because of the 'curse.'" While she didn't put air quotes around the word, her tone made her feelings clear.

"It almost sounds like you *don't* believe in the curse," I said cautiously.

She laughed, but it was a sour and acrid sound. "Oh, I most definitely believe in curses. Mostly because *they* believe. It's like that old quote, whether you believe you can do something or not, you're right." She turned to the window, her jaw tightening. "And boy, do the 1888ers believe in that curse."

For a moment, I just studied her. With her head turned toward the window, which hid the puffiness of her eyes, I could see her beauty. She could practically pass as a model, with her long, elegant neck and graceful profile. Again, I wondered how she found herself in Redemption, Wisconsin, and not just that, but in the poorest, least desirable part of Redemption. "I guess I'm still not clear how you're connected to the 1888ers."

She finally turned her head to look at me. "Isn't it obvious? Arthur is an 1888er."

"Oh." Of course. I should have figured that out myself. Except … how did someone who grew up believing he was cursed and would never amount to anything manage to marry a woman like the one seated across from me?

Again, it was as if she read my mind. "I was young, and I thought I was in love. We both did." She let out that acrid-sounding laugh again, except now, it carried a tinge of sadness. "We met at Alpine Valley at a Grateful Dead concert. I was twenty-two, and deep in my rebellion period." She sighed and ran a hand roughly through her hair. "Arthur was older, nearly thirty, and I knew the moment I laid eyes on him that my father would hate him. And, at that time of my life, that was all that mattered." She shook her head, her eyes unfocused. "I took him home with me that night, and two months later, we eloped. Vegas, of course. Because that's what my father would have hated."

She leaned back in her seat and gave me a knowing look. "If you haven't figured it out by now, my family has money. A lot of it. And while my father would have happily disowned me if he could, it wasn't his decision. My grandmother had already set me up with a trust fund. So even though my father tried his best to convince me I should do something more … *productive* with my life, I was bound and determined to do the exact opposite. Which is where Arthur came in.

"To his credit, he tried to dissuade me from marrying him. He told me about the curse and tried to warn me that I really didn't want this life. But, like the idiot I was, I ignored everything he said and insisted things could be different. *We* could be different. Our love was so strong it was no match for a curse." She shook her head in disgust. "Needless to say, I really was an idiot."

"You could make the argument that we're all idiots when we're in love," I said.

Something unreadable flickered across her face. "True, but somehow, it doesn't make me feel any better." She turned away from me and grabbed a napkin to start dabbing at her eyes. "What a pair we were. Both of us with daddy issues. No wonder we were drawn to each other." The bitter note was back in her voice.

"What were Arthur's issues?" I asked.

She crumpled the napkin in her hand. "The bar." She practically spat out the words. "It had somehow limped along for generations. His grandfather founded it; then his dad took it over, and finally, Arthur got it. But it was always a disaster. Basically, always one step away from bankruptcy." She gave her head a quick shake and reached for her tea to take a sip, making a slight face. It was probably cold, by that point, and I tried to unobtrusively push the green ceramic pot in her direction so she could freshen it up. "He convinced me that the reason why 88 Spirits was always struggling was that it never got the investment it needed to succeed. So, like an idiot, I gave it to him."

"It didn't work, I take it?" I asked.

"That's an understatement. It was basically a black hole." She reached for the pot, her lips pressed into a straight line. "There was a reason why 88 Spirits was such a disaster, and that reason was Arthur. He was a terrible businessman. Just dreadful." Her eyes flicked up toward me. "I'm not opposed to giving free drinks every once in a while, especially if someone is down on their luck or has had an especially bad day. But in Arthur's mind, the sheer fact that you were an 1888er was cause for free drinks. 'But the curse,'" her voice mimicked Arthur's. "'How can I charge them when I know how much they're struggling to get by?' Never mind how much the bar was struggling to get by. 'And why do you care?' he'd ask. 'You can afford it.'"

She closed her eyes tightly and pressed her fingers against her temples, as if the memory physically pained her. After a few moments, she got herself back under control and opened her eyes. "In retrospect, I think the fact that he married into money was the worst mistake." Her voice was back to normal.

I looked at her in confusion. "Why would you say that?"

"Because I think the fact that he had access to money, and so many of his friends and neighbors didn't, made him feel guilty. While I don't think he ever would have made 88 Spirits a success, he was too big-hearted to run a business," her face softened at the word big-hearted, and for the first time, I got a glimpse of the love she had for her husband, "I don't think it would have been as bad as it got."

"What did you do?" I asked.

She shrugged. "What could I do? I funded it. For years. Until finally, I realized I couldn't anymore."

"That must have been difficult," I said.

She let out another one of those sharp laughs that didn't reflect any real humor. "Again, an understatement. That night, we had the biggest fight of our marriage."

"When was this?" I braced myself to hear that it was just a few weeks or maybe a month before. I had an uneasy feeling that this was the reason why she was in my kitchen less than a day after finding out her husband died in a fire started in a bar she had propped up and clearly hated. She wanted me to do damage control—to convince the police (and maybe the town) that this argument had nothing to do with what just happened.

But she surprised me. "About a year and a half ago."

"Oh," I said, trying to keep my expression neutral, but she must have read my face.

"It wasn't easy, but we worked through it," she said with a knowing expression on her face. "It helped when I went through my trust fund numbers. I think he was under the impression it was a bottomless source of money, but he eventually understood."

"I guess part of why I'm a little shocked is you just finished telling me what a bad business owner he was," I said. "But 88 Spirits is still in business, isn't it?"

"Barely," she said. "But yes. I was right in my assessment that once he realized he couldn't count on me bailing out the bar, he did clean up his act. Some." Her mouth twisted as if she had just eaten something sour. "But I don't think that was the only thing he did."

"What do you mean?" I sat up a little straighter, my nerve endings starting to tingle.

Her eyes shifted around the kitchen. "I think he got money from somewhere else."

"He did?" Again, I couldn't hide my surprise. "Where? I thought the 1888ers were broke."

"They are. The ones I know of, anyway." Her eyes narrowed. "But he didn't necessarily get it from them."

There was something dark in her voice that was making my skin crawl. "Where else would he go?"

"I can tell you where he didn't go." Her voice was flat. "A bank. Or any sort of above-board investment group."

Oh boy. "So you think it wasn't legal?"

"I don't see how it could be." She picked up her tea to take a sip. "Unless he somehow managed to figure out how to cook his books, or maybe hired someone to do it for him. No bank or reputable lender would have anything to do with that business."

If the way she described her husband's business was accurate, she was probably right. "Are you sure he got money from somewhere? Maybe he just learned to manage the business better."

She rolled her eyes. "I know my husband. Before he got the money, he was super uptight and stressed. Not sleeping or eating. But then, one day, he was relaxed again. Just like he would be after I'd give him money." She shook her head. "No, someone definitely helped him out. I don't know the particulars, but I'm sure it happened."

My head was whirling with all the information she'd given me. "Do you think whoever it was is behind the bar burning down?"

"Maybe," Carol said. She was still holding her mug, and I could see her hands start to tremble, sloshing tea out of it. But she didn't seem to notice. "If they're the kind of people who would be willing to lend my husband money, then yeah. I think it's very possible."

"We need to tell the police." I started to get up to call Wyle. This seemed like a solid lead he could dig into.

She let out a yelp. "No. No police."

I stopped, halfway out of my chair. "Why not?"

"It's too dangerous."

"What?" I couldn't believe I had heard her right.

Carol's hand snaked across the table to grab my arm. "Please, listen to me." Her eyes were desperate. "The cops … they're not going to do anything anyway. If they investigate, which is a big if, it will be half-hearted. And they certainly won't arrest anyone. Which means, if whoever lent Arthur the money gets wind that I'm the one who told the cops about them, they could come after me."

"I don't think that would happen," I said, sinking back down into my seat.

The look on her face was one of disgust and loathing, although who she was directing it toward, I wasn't sure. "You don't know. You didn't grow up here."

"Fair enough, but that's because it doesn't make any sense to me. Why won't the cops investigate?"

"Because they don't want anything to do with the 1888ers. Nobody does." She leaned forward, her eyes glittering. "Why would anyone choose to align themselves with a community that is convinced they are cursed, resulting in their lives sucking even more than normal? Anyone other than a lovesick twenty-year-old with daddy issues, that is." Her smile had turned self-mocking. "Arthur was right. I should have listened to him all those years ago."

I didn't think she meant it. I could hear the pain in her voice, and I suspected it was the grief talking. "It wasn't all bad, was it?"

My hope was that the question would bring her back to the happier times in her relationship, but it seemed to do the exact opposite. Her face darkened as she turned her head to look out the window. "No, it wasn't, but was it good enough to offset becoming part of a cursed community?" She didn't wait for an answer. "I'm sure it's probably coincidental, but of all my family members, I'm the one who had the most issues with my trust fund. Investments that have tanked—*real* investments, mind you, not 88 Spirits investments—embezzlements, yes plural, and one was just last summer! Quite frankly, I'm lucky to have any money left at all." She fiddled with one of her rings, a lovely emerald encircled by diamonds. "I know it's not possible, that curses aren't contagious, but … there are moments when I wonder if every single thing I've ever heard in this forsaken community is real. And now, some of their bad luck has rubbed off on me."

"I don't think that's how curses work," I said as my mind replayed Pat saying practically the same thing, word for word. But I was sure both Pat and Carol were wrong. Curses didn't exist, and even if they did, it wasn't like catching a cold. They didn't spread willy-nilly. They were a deliberate act. And in the case of Carol and her trust fund, if she had continued to fund her husband's bar long after realizing it had proven to be a failure, she probably made other mistakes that had caused her trust fund to dwindle, as well.

Probably.

"Maybe not," Carol said, running a hand roughly through her hair. "But regardless of curses being real or not, I think it would be best if I leave. Get as far away from here as possible." She smiled slightly. "Maybe California. If nothing else, the weather will certainly be better."

Considering it was yet another cold Wisconsin winter day, I had to agree. "That might not be the worst idea. Leaving and starting over somewhere fresh."

She was still focused on her ring, spinning it over and over again on her finger. "That's why I need your help. The sooner we know what happened to Arthur, the sooner I can sell my house and leave."

"I completely understand," I said as I reached for the pot to refill my own mug of tea. "But it seems to me that it might make more sense to talk to the police rather than me. After all, it doesn't really matter what I discover. I'm just a tea maker."

Her face darkened. "I already told you. It's a waste of time. The police aren't going to investigate."

"Yes, you said that, but this isn't a bar fight or a couple of kids shoplifting. This is potential arson and murder. The cops just can't ignore it. I don't care how much they don't want to deal with the 1888ers."

She let out a sigh and rubbed her nose between her eyes. "It's not just the cops. It's the 1888ers, as well."

"What do you mean?"

She dropped her hand and gave me a look like she couldn't believe I really was the one who had solved other tough cases. And for that matter, she was starting to regret coming to my house in the first place. "The 1888ers don't want anything to do with outsiders."

My mind flashed back to driving through the tiny community with its duplicate stores that were only a few miles away from their counterparts in Redemption proper. That had never made sense to me, even though I knew that area of town kept to itself. But at this point, I was starting to have a lot more sympathy for the 1888ers. "That doesn't sound all that surprising. If you knew people were afraid of being around because they thought they might become cursed, I can see why they would want to keep to themselves."

Carol shook her head. "That's not why. I mean, it's not the real reason. There might be some of that now, true, but it didn't start out that way."

"How did it start then?"

Carol hesitated, chewing on her bottom lip. Her lipstick, the only makeup she wore, had flaked off. She glanced around the kitchen as if she were afraid someone might overhear us, but other than Midnight, who was busy snoring in the sun, we were completely alone. "You have to understand," she said quietly, so quietly I had to lean forward slightly. "The 1888ers don't believe they did anything wrong."

I frowned. "I'm sorry?"

Her eyes were boring into mine. "So, as you probably know, no one knows for sure what happened in 1888, or why the adults disappeared. But a lot of people, especially the ones who live in Redemption but aren't 1888ers, believe that the adults were at least partly to blame for it. They must have done something, right? Because it's not natural for an entire population to simply vanish overnight. They must have done something to someone to make that happen.

"But that's not the only reason people get cursed. Look at fairytales and Greek mythology. Sure, sometimes people are cursed because they did something. Maybe just offended a witch or a god, which, according to the stories, is more than enough to get yourself cursed. But that wasn't always the case. Sometimes, people were cursed because that witch or god simply had it out for them. They could be jealous of someone's beauty or goodness or something."

"The 1888ers think they were cursed because … some witch was jealous of them?" Of all the stories and rumors I had heard over the few years I had lived in Redemption, I thought this was probably the least likely reason that would cause an entire population of adults to disappear.

She let out an exasperated sigh, again looking like she thought she'd made a huge mistake opening up to me. "That is just an example. Did you miss the part where I said no one knows what happened to the 1888ers? The point is, the 1888ers believe they were wrongly cursed, and because of that, they have trust issues. A lot of them. Especially when it comes to cops or …" she paused and started fiddling with her mug. "Well, anyone who isn't one of them."

"Makes sense," I said. "But if that's the case, and I'm not trying to be rude, but why are you here? I'm certainly not one of them, so I'm unclear what you're asking me to do."

Her face crumbled, and for a moment, I thought she was going to start to cry. "I know, but I don't know what else to do." She grabbed her napkin and pressed it to her eyes as she sucked in deep breaths.

I felt horrible. Here was a woman who had just lost her husband a day ago and had shown up on my doorstep because she needed help. And obviously, I wasn't helping. On the other hand, I wasn't sure what I was supposed to do. How was I supposed to investigate when it didn't appear as though anyone would be willing to talk to me? And what about the cops? Everyone, (well, everyone other than Wyle) seemed to be under the impression that the cops weren't going to do anything. Did Carol really think I would be able to step in and accomplish something the cops couldn't?

Carol got herself under control and dropped her hand so she could meet my gaze. "Charlie, I know what I'm asking is a lot. Too much, in fact. But I don't know what else to do. I'm desperate." She squeezed her fists together so tightly that her fingers began turning white. "There's too much I don't know about what happened yesterday. What if whoever set fire to 88 Spirits and killed my husband isn't done yet? What if I'm next?" Her breathing was ragged again as she squeezed her fists even tighter.

"Look, even if your husband did borrow money from some sketchy character, that doesn't mean they'll come after you," I said, starting to feel a little alarmed. Her skin was waxy and pale, and I was starting to worry she might have an anxiety attack. Or worse.

"You don't know that," she said, her voice going up a notch. "You don't know who these people are. If they know I have money, they might decide I am responsible for paying back Arthur's loan."

"Again, that's why you would probably be better off talking to the police," I said. "They have the resources to help you. I don't."

Her breathing became more erratic. "I told you. That's not an option. They're not going to do anything, and if they do, it will probably make things worse."

Under normal circumstances, I would have assumed Carol wasn't thinking straight because of grief. But my mind kept replaying the scene with Pat, Mildred, and Tilde all laughing at Wyle in my kitchen earlier that morning.

But it was even more than that. The cops had made it clear they had no interest in looking for a missing pregnant girl. Wyle aside, could I really be so sure the cops would do anything at all, if not that?

"It's not just my life and well-being I'm worried about," Carol said suddenly. Her voice was calmer, as if she had finally regained her composure. "It's Arthur, too. He deserves to have the truth out there. He …" she swallowed hard. "He did everything he could to help the 1888ers, and they took advantage of it. If he was killed because he got a shady loan so he could keep giving out free drinks, the 1888ers should know that." She clenched her fists again, but it seemed like it was more from anger now than fear. "I owe it to Arthur to get the truth out."

Carol was staring at me, her expression fierce and determined. In that moment, I could see what had likely attracted Arthur to her in the first place.

And I was also reminded of what everyone was saying—about the waitress who looked like she was more girl than woman, and the unborn child she was carrying.

"If I agree to help you," I said. "I'm going to need you to be honest with me."

Her eyes lit up, and her expression turned triumphant. She knew she had me. "Of course!"

"Even about things you may not want to talk about."

Her face didn't change. "You want to know about Edie, don't you?"

Chapter 7

For a moment, I could only stare at Carol. I hadn't expected her to be so blunt.

"Actually, yes. That would be a good place to start," I said.

If she understood that Edie would only be the beginning, she gave no indication of it. "I know what everyone has been saying." Her expression had flattened, and her eyes narrowed. "That my husband was having an affair with a woman half his age and got her pregnant."

"And did he?"

She raised her chin to glare at me. "Absolutely not. My husband loved me."

"I'm sure he did," I said, keeping my voice neutral. "And I'm not trying to upset you, but you do realize that people cheat on people they love all the time, right?"

She swallowed hard and turned her head toward the window. "It's not just that." Her voice was soft. "We wanted a baby. For years, we tried to have children, but ..." she shook her head as her voice caught, her eyes glistening with unshed tears. "We couldn't."

There was something so sad and final about the way she said those two little words. I could feel my heart break in a new way for this woman who had just walked through my door minutes before. Her pain was obvious, from the tightness in her jaw to the brokenness of her voice. I figured this was something she struggled with daily, but now, with the loss of her husband so fresh, she felt it that much more acutely. She would never have children with her husband. That door was permanently shut.

I cleared my throat. "I'm so sorry." There didn't seem to be much else to say.

She inclined her head briefly in response. There was an awkward silence for a moment before I broke it.

"Can you describe what happened before the fire?"

She reached for a napkin to dab at her eyes before straightening up and turning to face me. "What do you want to know?"

"Oh, everything." I gave her a slanted smile, trying to soften my words. "I know this isn't an easy time, but the more you can tell me, the more helpful it will be."

She nodded. "It started like any other day. Arthur didn't get up until after nine, but that's normal when you own a bar and don't get home until after one in the morning. We had coffee together, which is also normal, although as I'm always up before him, I'd be on my third or fourth cup by then." She hesitated as she started playing with her tea mug again. "We were supposed to run some errands together, but he told me he had some paperwork he had to get done. I … I wasn't happy about it." Her face was flushed slightly. "We … we had some words about it."

"You had an argument?"

"Not exactly an argument … more like a disagreement." She took a deep, shaky breath. "I'm going to have to live with that for the rest of my life. My last interaction with him was centered around how unhappy I was that he was spending all his time working."

"That's tough. I'm sorry," I said quietly.

She gave me a brief nod and went back to playing with her mug. "Anyway, I decided to go ahead and run the errands on my own, so I took a shower and got ready. When I left, he was still in his office."

"So, you don't know when he went to the bar?" I asked.

She shook her head. "No. The last I saw him, he was still sitting at his desk."

"What time did you leave?"

She thought for a moment. "Around eleven. I remember thinking I would treat myself to lunch rather than eat at home." Pain fluttered across her face. "Originally, I had thought Arthur and I would have lunch together while we did errands, so I figured I'd go myself even if Arthur wasn't with me." A muscle jerked in her jaw, and she turned away, as if to get herself back under control.

"Anyway," she said after a moment, "by the time I got back to the house, Arthur was gone."

"What time was that?"

She screwed up her face. "I'm not sure. Around two, two thirty maybe? It could have been later. I didn't look at the time." She held out her arms. "And I don't wear a watch."

So, it sounded like she got home roughly around the time the fire started. I wondered if she had seen anything while she was running her errands. "Is your house near 88 Spirits?"

She pursed her lips. "It depends on your definition of 'near.' We're about a half-mile away or so."

"Did you happen to drive by the bar when you were out and about?"

"Not really. I took a different way." She lifted her head and gave me a sharp look. "What are you saying? That if I had driven by 88 Spirits, I might have been able to prevent what happened?"

"Well, I don't know about that," I said quickly. "I was just trying to cover all the bases." She had such a horrified look on her face, I didn't have the heart to tell her that it was possible she might have seen something if she had driven by at the right time.

Her breathing had gone ragged, and she pressed a hand to her chest. "I didn't even think about that … that I might have been able to do something to stop …" her voice trailed off, and she gripped a handful of her sweater.

"It would have been a long shot," I said. "I truly doubt you could have stopped anything. I'm just trying to get as much information as possible. When did Arthur normally go to the bar?"

She was still squeezing her sweater with her fist. "It depends," she said, blinking a few times.

"Depends on what?"

"On what he had to do that day. Some tasks were just easier to do at the bar rather than from his home office."

"Did he usually work at home?"

She made a face. "No. That was another thing we fought about. Part of the reason why we set up a home office in the first place was so he could spend more time at home, but all it seemed to do was to extend his workday. Rather than going into the bar sometime after lunch, he would spend the morning at home working before heading over in the afternoon."

My heart sank. I had been hoping Carol could at least give me a timeframe to work with, beginning when Arthur left the house, and maybe even some idea as to what he had been doing. But it sounded as if she were as clueless as the rest of us. "So you have no idea when he went in or what he could have been working on?"

"No. All I know is he was in his office when I left around eleven …" her voice trailed off, and her eyes glazed over. "Actually, there is something."

I leaned forward, my spine starting to tingle. "What?"

She sucked in a deep breath. "Arthur had taken a phone call. I was still upstairs getting ready, so I couldn't hear the exact words, but I could hear Arthur's tone."

"What was his tone?"

Her eyes cut toward me. "He was stressed. That was clear. But there was something more. Almost like an … urgency to his voice."

"Urgency?"

She cocked her head as if she were replaying Arthur's voice. "Maybe it was more like … desperation."

"He was desperate?" My mind went back to what she'd said about Arthur borrowing money from unsavory people. "Why?"

"I don't know." But her expression was uneasy.

"Did you ask him about it?"

She looked alarmed. "Oh no. He would have been furious if he thought I was listening in on his business conversations. Especially since …" she glanced toward the window again. "Especially since I was no longer giving the business money. That was one of our agreements—if I wasn't going to be an *investor*," she rolled her eyes at the word, "then I wasn't going to ask any questions about the business. At the time, I was delighted to agree to it. Our only arguments were about 88 Spirits, so I was happy to never discuss it with Arthur ever again." Her expression turned sad. "What I didn't realize, or at least fully comprehend, was how that bar had become Arthur's life, and if we couldn't talk about it, well … we didn't have much to talk about."

She looked so unhappy that I was starting to wish I didn't have to ask my next questions, but if she truly wanted me to investigate her husband's death, I had no choice. "What about Edie?"

It was as if I had thrown cold water on her. She jerked up and met my gaze, eyes narrowing slightly. "What about her?"

"Do you know why she was at the bar with Arthur?"

She drew herself up even more. "I assume she had to work."

"When did the bar open?" Between the lack of cars in the parking lot and the lack of response to the fire, I had figured the bar was closed. But if it was, why would a waitress be there, working?

"Usually by three or four. Sometimes a little earlier. He definitely wanted to catch the after-work crowd, but he didn't want to sit there in an empty bar all afternoon, either."

So it was possible the bar had just opened, or was about to open, when the fire started. Which opened up the possibility that maybe a customer or two had seen something.

Of course, if that were the case, why hadn't the fire department been called sooner? Unless they had to go find a phone somewhere. I tried to picture where the nearest pay phone was, but I couldn't remember seeing one.

"I'm sorry I can't help you more," Carol was saying, and I gave myself a quick mental shake. I could work out the timing later. "But you'll keep me informed of your progress, yes?" She gave me an expectant look

"Um ..." I still wasn't sure this was a good idea. Pat's warning continued ringing in my ears. However, I had just spent the last twenty minutes asking her a bunch of uncomfortable questions, so I really couldn't say no now.

"And you'll also send me an invoice for your fee?" She had started to rise.

"Oh, I don't ..." I started to say, but she waved me off.

"I insist."

I had no plans to send her an invoice, but I didn't feel like wasting time arguing about it. "Are you sure there's nothing else you can share? I'm not even entirely sure where to start."

She paused and turned toward me, a brittle sort of smile on her lips. Her eyes were red-rimmed, and it hit me that this woman who had just lost her husband was not only dealing with her grief but also with a lot of ugly rumors, and possibly even a threat to her own life. It would be a lot for anyone. "I'm confident you'll figure it out," she said.

Chapter 8

It was a cold but bright and sunny morning when I parked the car next to the curb in front of Hattie's house. After Carol had left the day before, I'd spent the evening trying to figure out a game plan. Unfortunately, calling Pat, which is what I would normally do, was off the table. Wyle would be my second choice, but I was hesitant to talk to him as well, and not just because I didn't want a lecture about leaving the investigation to the professionals. I wasn't sure how much I could trust the Redemption Police Department. Wyle, I absolutely trusted, but the rest of the department? I wasn't sure.

So after spending the night racking my brain, I could think of only two people who might be able to help: Mildred and Hattie.

Neither were ideal. While Hattie was an 1888er and presumably would at least know who I could talk to, I had no idea how she would react if I started asking her questions. Would she get upset and throw me out of her house? It was possible. The 1888ers did seem to be a squirrelly bunch. And while it wouldn't make any difference to me if I stopped selling her tea, I would feel bad for her, as I knew how much pain she was in and how much she said my tea helped her.

As for Mildred ... well, that was always a crapshoot. Who knew how Mildred would react? But she at least had 1888ers as students, so if anyone outside of the tight-knit community would know who I should talk to, it would be her.

Hattie seemed like the best bet, so I decided to start with her.

I rang the doorbell and waited. And waited. And waited.

She normally took a bit of time to answer the door, as her arthritis made it difficult for her to walk, so I was prepared for that. But this seemed a little much, even for Hattie.

Was she not at home? No, Hattie was always home, especially this time of year, with the cold. Was she not up? I glanced at my watch. It was after ten—early, but not that early. She should be up and about.

Had something happened to her?

My stomach churned. What should I do? I didn't know any other 1888er, so I had no idea who might have a key to Hattie's house. Should I break in? I hated to do that, but what choice did I have? I couldn't leave her in there knowing something might be very wrong, and I suspected if it was a choice between me or the police, she would prefer me.

Thankfully, before it got to that point, I heard the sound of the door being unlocked.

"Oh, Charlie." Hattie tried to smile at me through the crack of the door, but it fell flat. Her short gray hair, which was normally carefully brushed, was standing on end, as if she had just gotten out of bed. Her bright-pink sweatshirt had what looked like a coffee stain on it, which was also strange—while she never dressed up, everything she wore was always neat and clean. "What are you doing here?"

I smiled brightly, holding up a tea bag. "I had some extra tea, and I thought I would just stop by and give it to you rather than wait until your next order."

"Oh." She hesitated, her eyes shifting. "You didn't have to do that."

"I know." I waved the bag. "Can I come in?"

Again, her eyes shifted to the side. "Um … it's not really a good time."

My smile faded as I slowly lowered the bag. "Hattie, is someone in there with you?"

Her eyes went wide. "What? No. Why would you say that?" Except the expression on her face inferred the exact opposite.

I lowered my voice. "Hattie, are you in danger?"

Her eyes, a light, watery blue, were still wide. "No, no, no. Of course not. Don't be silly." She let out a laugh, but it sounded a little hysterical.

I reached up and gently pushed the door open, not wanting to knock her over, but I was determined to get in. I had no idea what was going on, but between Carol telling me about Arthur's possible involvement with some shady characters and whatever actually happened at 88 Spirits, I didn't want to take any chances. "Let me in, Hattie. It's too cold for you to be standing in front of the door like this."

"Oh, no, Charlie. You shouldn't bother," Hattie fretted, but she stepped back enough to let me in. The front door opened to the living room, which was on the left, and the kitchen down the hall. To the right, in the back, was a bedroom and a bathroom. I caught a faint whiff of eggs, toast, and coffee mixed with the musty scent of dust (Hattie did her best—her house was neat, but not necessarily clean) as I shut the door behind me.

"What's going on?" I asked, turning to her.

She took another step back, folding her arms across her chest. "Nothing. I don't know what you're talking about."

"Hattie, I know I'm … an outsider, but you know me. You can trust me. What's going on?"

"I …" She licked her lips, a haunted expression on her face. "You shouldn't be here. It doesn't concern you."

"Let me be the judge of that."

She shook her head. "No. It's not safe. You should …"

There was a crash coming from the kitchen. Hattie jumped, letting out a little cry.

"Who's here?" I demanded.

Hattie just stared at me, shaking her head.

I strode down the hall, past the sparsely furnished living room with a small pile of folded blankets and a pillow on the faded green couch, and into the kitchen.

The first thing I noticed was that there were still remnants of breakfast strewn about: a pan on the stove with leftover scrambled eggs, a piece of toast on a plate, and a jar of grape jam with a butter knife still in it. The coffee pot was half-full, and there was a teapot next to it.

And crouched on the floor, picking up broken pieces of what appeared to be a coffee cup, was Edie.

***

"How did you find me?" Edie asked. We were sitting around the scarred and faded kitchen table, cups of coffee in front of us. After I had swooped in to help Edie off the floor and into a chair, I cleaned up the mess. Then, the three of us gathered around the table.

Edie definitely looked a lot better than when I had last seen her. Her sandy brown hair was clean and pulled back in a ponytail, and her dark-blue eyes were only slightly bloodshot. Her face was puffy, and she did have dark circles under her eyes, but that could have been attributed to the pregnancy rather than the fire. She wore a white tee shirt that was way too small for her and didn't cover her stomach at all with a zippered gray sweatshirt that hung open and gray drawstring pants that strained over her swollen belly. I was fairly certain each was from Hattie's closet.

"I've known Hattie for a couple of years," I said, which didn't answer the question. "Carol asked me to look into the fire." I studied Edie as I picked up my coffee, especially curious how she would react to Carol's name.

Her eyes darted toward mine as something that looked like guilt slid over her face. "Did you tell her where I was?"

Interesting reaction. "How could I tell her where you were when I didn't know until five minutes ago?"

Her jaw tightened. "Are you going to tell her?"

"Why don't you want me to tell her where you are?" I countered. Was she having an affair after all? I hadn't wanted to believe it, but now, I wasn't so sure.

Edie looked down into her untouched coffee. "It's complicated."

Oh geez. This was not looking good. "What's complicated?" I kept my tone calm and nonthreatening, hoping she would bring up Arthur on her own.

For a moment, she didn't answer, choosing instead to fidget with her coffee cup. But finally, she tilted her head toward me to eye me. "I'm sure you've heard the rumors … that I'm sleeping with Arthur, and he's the father of my baby." She rubbed her belly protectively as she said it.

"Are you?"

Her eyes narrowed, and her lips pursed in disgust. "No! He's way too old for me." She swallowed hard and ducked her head. "Was, I mean."

I believed her. Her outburst was too honest and raw. And that look of disgust didn't look staged. Maybe I would come to find out she was a terrific actress, but at least for now, I thought she was telling the truth.

"If you weren't, then why does everyone think you were?" I asked.

"Because everyone's minds are in the gutter," she snapped, except again, she wasn't meeting my eyes.

"While I don't disagree, there has to be something more to it," I said. "Surely, you weren't the first waitress who worked for Arthur to get pregnant. And what about the father?"

"He's not in the picture." Her voice was flat as she turned away to stare out the window.

"I'm sorry to hear that," I said. Even though it wasn't any of my business, I was itching to ask more questions, but the closed-down expression on her face made it clear she wouldn't answer. "And you and Arthur …"

"We were friends." Her tone was still flat. "That was it. There was nothing between us. He was helping me."

Something jangled inside me as I leaned forward slightly. "How was he helping you?"

Hattie reached forward to touch my hand. "It's not important."

I looked at her in confusion. "Of course it's important. A man is dead."

"But it could have been an accident," Hattie insisted as all the blood seemed to drain from Edie's face.

"If it was an accident, then why is Edie hiding at your house?" I asked.

Hattie reared back as if I had slapped her. "Edie is not hiding here."

I raised my eyebrows. "Oh? Does anyone else know she's here?"

Hattie looked uncomfortable. "Well, no …"

"Then how is it not hiding?"

"It just isn't," Hattie insisted. "Edie is here because I've got the room and am happy to have the company."

"Then why not tell people?" I asked.

"Because there's no one to tell," Hattie said.

I raised an eyebrow. "No one to tell? She survived a fire. I would think someone would be worried about her."

"You're making a bigger deal out of this than it is," Hattie said.

This was starting to get ridiculous. "So there's no reason why all of Redemption shouldn't know Edie is staying here?"

"Well, it's none of their business," Hattie sniffed. Edie, for her part, simply looked horrified.

"If someone is worried about Edie, I think it would be their business," I said. "And the cops would certainly think it was their business."

Hattie's eyes hardened. "It's certainly not the cops' business."

"As they're in the middle of investigating what caused the fire, I'm sure they would disagree."

"I told you, it was an accident."

How was this conversation real? The longer it went on, the more insane it was getting. "Was it an accident that caused the back door to be blocked so no one could get out?" My voice came out harsher than I intended, but I needed to get through to them. The more they kept tap dancing around the issue, the more I was certain there was something rotten going on, and Edie, Hattie, Carol, and maybe others, too, could very well be in danger.

But almost as soon as the words were out of my mouth, I regretted them. Well, almost. Hattie gasped, pressing a hand to her chest, and for a moment, I was afraid she might be having a heart attack.

Edie's face had gone so pale and chalky, I was also a little afraid for the baby. The last thing I wanted was either of them ending up in the hospital.

Although … if this was that upsetting to them, I was probably on the right track.

"Charlie, you shouldn't …" Hattie shook her head before lowering her voice. "You shouldn't say such things."

"But why?" I asked in my normal voice.

Hattie's head snapped back, like I had been shouting, and she started gesturing wildly for me to lower my voice. "Not so loud."

Bewildered, I looked around the kitchen, seeing if there was maybe someone hiding behind the fridge. "It's just us, right? Or is there someone else in here?"

"There are no other *people* here," Hattie said. "But that doesn't mean we're alone."

"You're never alone in Redemption," Edie said darkly.

Again, I looked around the kitchen, this time studying the windows to see if anyone was pressed up against the glass. "I know it's a small town, but I think we're probably safe here."

Edie gave me an almost pitying look. "It doesn't matter where we are. Redemption is always listening."

Even though I knew what she said was ridiculous, cold shivers shot up my spine. *I must be under a draft*, I thought. "Redemption is a town," I said firmly, although I did lower my voice. "It can't listen."

Edie's eyes flicked up toward me. "You sure about that?"

Again, I felt that cold shiver, except this time, it was at the back of my neck. I shifted uneasily in my chair and picked up my coffee, more for the heat than anything else. "Why don't you tell me what's really going on? What are you afraid of?"

Edie and Hattie exchanged a glance I couldn't read. "Honestly, Charlie, you're better off not knowing," Hattie said.

"That may be so," I said. "But I'm here, and I'm involved now, whether anyone likes it or not."

Again, Hattie and Edie looked at each other. "It's dangerous," Hattie said, although she sounded resigned.

"If it's dangerous for me, it's dangerous for you, as well," I said as I gestured at Edie. "Not to mention the baby."

"Yeah, but we don't have a lot of choice in the matter," Edie said. "You do."

"I can take care of myself," I said. "And besides, even if I wanted to stay out of it, I keep getting dragged in, so you might as well tell me."

There was a long pause as Hattie and Edie remained silent. "She's probably going to find out anyway," Edie finally said to Hattie. "I don't think we can stop it. And maybe it's better if she knows, so she can protect herself."

Hattie let out a sigh. "I suppose you're right." She turned to me, her face almost gray. "Are you sure? There's no turning back."

"I'm sure," I said, but even as I said it, I wondered if I was. Despite telling Edie and Hattie the truth about it seeming like I had no choice but to investigate, a part of me wondered if I was making a big mistake. I wondered if I should just stand up, walk out, and go home to call Carol to tell her I couldn't help her after all.

But even as I contemplated it, I knew I wouldn't leave. I was in too deep. No matter where this went, I had to see it through to the end.

Hattie nodded, as if she knew that would be my answer. "Okay then." She took a deep breath. "Do you know why we're called the 1888ers?"

"Yes, because you are descendants of the children of the adults who disappeared," I said.

"So you know we're cursed," Edie said, her voice bitter.

Hattie shook her head and reached out to squeeze Edie's hand. "It doesn't have to be that way, dear. Things can change."

Edie's face was pale, and her skin seemed to be stretched too thin around her eyes and mouth. "I don't know if I believe that anymore. Not after ..." Her voice trailed off, and she made a gulping noise, as if she was trying to swallow her tears.

Even though I was still inclined to believe her that she hadn't had an affair with Arthur, I was beginning to understand why the rumors had started.

Hattie patted her hand. "Don't blame yourself. Arthur wouldn't."

Edie hung her head. "He should. It's all my fault."

"Of course it isn't," Hattie said, clucking her tongue. "Don't say such nonsense."

"What do you think was your fault?" I asked. Was it possible Edie had done something to start the fire? Even if she had, there was no way that piece of wood could have magically ended up blocking the door. No matter what Wyle said, that was no accident.

"It's *not* her fault," Hattie said, giving me a stern look.

"I didn't say it was," I said. "I asked what she thinks is her fault."

Edie finally raised her head. Her eyes were red-rimmed, and she scrubbed at her face with her hands. "It's my fault Arthur's dead. Because he was protecting me."

"What was he protecting you from?" Maybe this was the connection to whoever lent Arthur the money.

Edie glanced at Hattie, who gave her a tight nod, before turning back to me. "The Forgotten."

Chapter 9

It felt like the temperature in the room dropped twenty degrees. I shivered as I hugged myself, my entire body covered with goose-bumps. Was there something wrong with Hattie's heat? Did I dare say anything? Even though she lived pretty simply, I didn't think she was as poor as some of the 1888ers, so I doubted her heat would have been turned off because of nonpayment. Of course, there could have been a mix-up, but I didn't think that very likely in the middle of winter in Wisconsin.

Still, I couldn't shake the feeling that there was something wrong. The uneasiness uncurled in the pit of my stomach as I was thrust back into my dream, surrounded by fire with no hope of escape. The smell of soot and ash in my nostrils. The faint echo of the sound of a curse.

Oh geez. Where did that come from? I gave myself a quick shake and forced myself to focus on the present. The Forgotten had nothing to do with my dreams. If anything, I should be focused on how it's a very odd name for a loan-shark operation.

Luckily for me, neither Hattie nor Edie noticed anything strange in my behavior. Edie was back to playing with her coffee cup, and Hattie was busy sighing. She looked as if she had aged twenty years since she had first sat down at the table.

"The Forgotten?" I asked.

Hattie was the one who answered, but she didn't look at me. "The easiest way to understand this is to think of the 1888ers as two factions. One faction, the majority, I might add, believe that while the curse isn't their fault, there isn't much they can do about it. For them, they do their best to live their lives despite the curse."

She paused and swallowed hard, her skin now a strange, un-healthy shade of gray. "The second faction, however, has different ideas. They believe the curse was more of a ... side effect, per se. That the reason our ancestors disappeared is that they either knowingly or unknowingly tapped into a … a great power. And if they could tap into that power again, they could not only reverse the curse, but become anything they want."

I blinked. Okay, this didn't sound anything like a loan-shark operation. Tendrils of my dream uneasily curled around me, and I batted them away, telling myself I was being silly. "What do you mean, 'a great power'?"

Edie opened her mouth to answer, but Hattie gave her a quick shake of her head. "The less said, the better," Hattie said darkly. "Trust me. You don't want to catch their attention."

I shivered again. Icy fingers were crawling down my spine. It was true that there were a lot of unexplained things that happened in Redemption, and most people blamed Redemption's strange and disturbing history.

But I wondered now if there was something more to it.

Or if there was really just an issue with Hattie's furnace.

"How does The Forgotten do that?" I asked.

Hattie pressed her lips together in a straight line. "Who knows, but whatever it is, I'm sure it's nothing good. I don't know any particulars. No one does."

"Do you know who they are?" I asked.

Edie and Hattie looked at each other again. "There's not a lot of them," Hattie said, which didn't answer the question. "The vast majority of 1888ers either try to stay far away from them or convince them to leave well enough alone. They tend to be young, and typically, it's a phase they outgrow."

"What happens when they outgrow it?" I asked. "They become like … regular 1888ers?"

Edie's mouth twisted into a sour expression. "You have no idea what it's like," she said as she glared at me, although it didn't feel like it was me she was upset with.

"It doesn't have to be that way," Hattie said gently.

Edie looked down at the table, her mouth working. "You don't understand."

"I do understand," Hattie said. "I was young once myself, although I realize it was a long time ago. There's always a choice in how you respond to bad things."

I tilted my head to study Hattie. "What was your choice?"

She answered immediately. "To live my life and not worry about the curse. Bad things happen to everyone, not just to us. We can always choose joy and peace."

Edie muttered something that sounded like "easy for you to say," but she kept her head down, so it was difficult to tell.

"Is that why you bought tea from me?" I asked. I had been wondering about her reasoning ever since the conversation between Pat, Wyle, Tilde, and Mildred.

She smiled, a real smile, and for the first time that morning, some healthy color returned to her face. "As I said, it's a choice. I never agreed with the isolationist tendencies of my fellow 1888ers. I know that puts me at odds with some of them, but …" she shrugged. "It's their loss. And I know a few who could really use the benefits of your tea."

"If it would help, I could give you extra, and you could just … slip it to some of them." I couldn't help it, as I truly hated the idea of 1888ers suffering from ailments my tea could help with.

Her smile turned sad. "I wish it were as easy as that."

A part of me wanted to keep asking her questions to see if I could convince her to at least try, but I knew this wasn't the time. Once this investigation was over, I could revisit the topic with Hattie. In the meantime, I needed to focus on what happened to Arthur.

"What does The Forgotten have to do with 88 Spirits burning down?" I asked, shifting the subject.

"They're bullies," Hattie said, her hands fluttering around her face. There was a hint of disgust in her voice, but it sounded almost forced. "Who knows why they decide to do the things they do?"

"It's more than that," Edie said. Her voice was quiet, but there was strength in it.

Hattie whipped her head toward Edie. "You don't have to say anything," she said before quickly turning back to me. "Charlie, you just have to trust me. There are things you're better off not knowing."

"But ..."

"It's okay, Hattie," Edie said, reaching out to give Hattie's hand a squeeze before straightening up and looking directly at me. "Arthur deserves the truth." She paused to take an unsteady breath. "He was protecting me from The Forgotten."

There was a loud bang, making us all jump. Automatically, I leaped up and headed to the kitchen window to look out. It sounded like a bird had hit the glass, and it was loud enough that I assumed it would have fallen to the ground, either dead or stunned. If it was stunned, I wanted to get it off the snow and somewhere safe for it to recover.

But there was nothing there. The snow was smooth and untouched as far as I could see. No sign that anything had been outside.

"I told you." Hattie's voice was ominous from behind me. I turned to see her clutching her pink sweatshirt with one hand, her face bloodless. "Redemption is listening."

I went back to my chair, trying to ignore the chills dancing along my spine. "I'm sure it was just a bird. Luckily, it didn't hurt itself, because it flew away."

Hattie's eyes were hooded as she stared at me. "If it had been a bird, you would have seen it in the snow."

Despite myself, I shivered. "Not necessarily. I've heard bangs just as loud and seen the birds fly away."

Hattie didn't blink. "If you say so."

I looked away. There was something so eerie about the way Hattie sat there, so still, it was making me uneasy. I focused on Edie, instead, who had a peculiar expression on her face. "Why was Arthur protecting you from The Forgotten?"

She didn't react, as if she were so deep in thought, she hadn't heard me. I was about to repeat my question when she roused herself, blinking as if she had woken from a deep sleep. "Because they wanted something from me."

"What did they want?"

"It doesn't matter." She shot me a look of disdain as she tossed her head, her hair bouncing around in its ponytail. In that moment, I could see the teenager she had once been.

"I think it matters a lot, if they were willing to burn down a bar for it," I said.

Edie blanched, and Hattie shot me a hard look. "For heaven's sake, Charlie! Don't you think she feels bad enough?"

"This isn't about feelings. It's about getting to the bottom of what happened, so we can keep you both safe," I said.

"Telling you isn't going to keep us safe," Edie said.

"Was it money?"

Edie blinked at me, looking genuinely surprised. "What?"

"Money. Did The Forgotten loan you money?"

"What would make you think that?" Hattie asked, looking just as perplexed.

"Because money tends to be at the root of a lot of crime," I said. "Plus, someone loaned Arthur money, and I was wondering if it might be The Forgotten."

So much for hoping to shock the truth out of either of them. They were both looking at me as if I had just sprouted a second head.

"Someone loaned Arthur money?" Edie asked.

"That's what Carol says," I said.

"Do you know anything about this?" Hattie asked, turning to Edie.

Edie sat back in her chair, a puzzled look on her face. "No, but …" Her eyes went to the ceiling as she thought. "You know, now that you say it, I think you must be right. He did get some money from somewhere."

I leaned forward in my chair. "Why do you say that?"

"Because he hasn't been stressed about money," Edie said. "When Carol was an investor-" At that, I pressed my lips tightly together to keep from laughing. All I could imagine was Carol's face, being called an "investor" in 88 Spirits. "Arthur was a lot more relaxed and happier. But when she pulled out …" She shook her head, making a disapproving face. "It wasn't a very nice thing to do to him."

"According to Carol, she did it because the bar was losing money hand over fist."

"It was running smoothly," Edie insisted. "She just doesn't understand how business works. She's never even had a job before."

While that was undoubtedly true, it sounded more like Arthur's excuses than anything else. "Do you have any idea who would have lent him money?"

Edie furrowed her brow as she thought. "Arthur dealt with a lot of different people. I didn't know them all, but … it's certainly possible he found some different investors who understood the bar business better than Carol. A lot of people liked him. He had a lot of friends."

"Everyone in the community liked him," Hattie said. "Even I liked him, and it's been a few years since I was able to have a drink at 88 Spirits. I'm sure if he asked around, he could have found someone to chip in."

I suspected the reason he had so many "friends" was because of all the free booze he gave out. "Was anyone upset with Arthur?"

Edie gave me a baffled look. "Why would anyone be upset with Arthur? We just told you, everyone loved him. This has nothing to do with him, other than …" her face closed in on itself. "Other than his trying to help me."

Hattie reached over to squeeze her hand again. "It's not your fault, dear. Arthur would agree."

She gave her head a quick shake but didn't answer.

I gave her a moment to gather herself before continuing. "So, if it wasn't money that The Forgotten wanted from you, what was it?"

Edie frowned. "I told you, it doesn't matter. The point is, what they want isn't theirs, and I have no intention of giving it to them. And Arthur agreed with me."

"So you're really saying The Forgotten were willing to burn down a bar because you didn't give them what they wanted?"

"They're used to getting what they want," Edie said, but she had a strange expression on her face as if hearing me say it made her realize how ridiculous she sounded.

"Do you know for sure it was The Forgotten?"

Her face hardened. "Do you mean do I have proof? Of course not. But …" She paused, biting her bottom lip. "Before the fire, I was in the basement getting supplies stocked for that night. I didn't know anyone else was here, other than Arthur, until I was back in the kitchen. And that's when I heard …" Her face twisted, and her eyes went glassy. "I heard Arthur arguing with someone."

I leaned forward. "Who?"

She shook her head. "I didn't hear the other person. I didn't even hear much of what Arthur said, except for the end. He said …" she turned away, still biting her lip. "He said, 'I already told you, she's not here. You know you're not welcome here, so please leave.'"

Oh, man. No wonder why she thought this was all her fault. "And by 'she,'" I said slowly, "you think he meant …"

"Me." She turned back to me, her eyes blinking wildly as if to stop the tears from falling. "Who else would it be?"

She started sniffling again, and Hattie leaned forward to put an arm around her. She leaned against Hattie and struggled to get herself under control.

Watching her, I felt terrible for pushing, but what other choice did I have? Edie's life could be in danger. "Why would Arthur say they knew they weren't welcome?"

She straightened up, reaching for a napkin to blow her nose. "The Forgotten had come in a few times before, but Arthur always threw them out. The last time, he threatened to call …" her voice trailed off as she eyed Hattie, who had her lips pressed together. "Well, it doesn't matter who, but it worked. They haven't been back since. At least until … well …" She looked away, blinking back tears again.

I gave her another moment to let her compose herself. "So then what?"

She reached for a napkin to blow her nose. "I'm not really sure. Obviously, I stayed back there, waiting for whoever it was to go away. I was hoping they wouldn't come back, but …" she shook her head. "Anyway, I was still back there when I started to smell smoke. By the time I made it out to the main bar, the fire was raging. I was yelling for Arthur, but he didn't answer. I thought maybe he was upstairs, which is where his office was, and I was going to go get him, but the fire was already there. So I ran to the back door, instead, thinking I would get out and call someone to come find him. But I couldn't get the door open, so I backtracked to the window, with the stupid idea of breaking it and crawling out." She gestured toward her belly as she shook her head. "And that's when you showed up." She lifted her head and looked me directly in the eyes. "Thank you. I didn't say it before, and I should have, but thank you for saving my life, along with …" she rubbed her belly, gesturing with her head.

"Of course, but I didn't do anything that anyone else wouldn't have done," I said. "I only wish I could have done more." I didn't add for Arthur, but the way Edie's face twisted up, I knew she was thinking the same thing.

"Now do you see?" Hattie asked me after clearing her throat. "Do you see why there's nothing to be done, and we just have to move forward as best we can?"

I didn't see that at all. But looking at both Hattie's and Edie's grief-stricken but determined expressions, I wasn't sure if I was going to be able to convince either one of them differently.

Chapter 10

Alas, I was right. It didn't matter what I said; neither Hattie nor Edie would tell me anything more about that day, or even the identities of The Forgotten.

"You're better off not knowing," Hattie kept insisting.

"Besides, I already told you I couldn't hear their voices," Edie chimed in. "It could have been any one of them."

Which apparently meant there was a group of The Forgottens. I tried to find out how many were in it, but they wouldn't even tell me that.

"There's no way to know how many there are," Hattie said, her voice dismissive.

"You know, while this unknown number of The Forgottens are running around, neither of you is safe," I said.

Their expressions were identical as they stared at me. Unyielding, yet I could see the fear in their eyes. "We'll be fine," Hattie said, even though she didn't look like she would be fine. "1888ers take care of their own."

"What are you talking about?" I asked, exasperated. "The 1888ers just let a bar burn down and a man die."

Hattie swallowed hard, but her gaze was steely. "We take care of our own. Sometimes, things get out of control …"

I rolled my eyes. "That's an understatement."

Hattie continued as if I hadn't interrupted. "But we WILL deal with this ourselves. This isn't the first time something like this has happened, and it won't be the last."

"Besides," Edie said, her voice quiet, but I could still hear the edge. "Even if we told you, there's nothing you could do about it anyway."

That might be true, but I also thought I was far more able to defend myself than both an older woman who was so riddled with arthritis, she couldn't even clean her house properly and a heavily pregnant young woman.

But it didn't seem to matter what I said. Their minds were made up.

"So what about my coat?" I finally asked Edie in exasperation. If I couldn't get anywhere helping them with this investigation, maybe I could at least get my coat back.

Edie, for her part, at least had the grace to look ashamed. "That wasn't planned," she muttered, looking even more embarrassed. "And I was going to give your coat back to you. And pay you back."

"You can keep the money, but I would like my coat back," I said before taking another look at her makeshift too-small outfit. "Unless you still need it."

"No, I have a coat she can have," Hattie said. "It's too big for me, and I never wear it. I've been meaning to give it away."

If it was too big for Hattie, it would probably work for Edie. At least I hoped so, after giving Edie's makeshift outfit another dubious look.

After I cleared the table and washed the dishes (over both of their protest, but they were also too exhausted to deal with the mess in the kitchen, and I still felt like I needed to do something for them, even though I was pretty sure that feeling was misguided), Hattie walked me to the door. "I knew that coat was yours the moment she showed up," Hattie confided as we walked, keeping her voice low. "I figured you wouldn't be far behind. But Charlie …" her eyebrows knitted together. "You really need to leave this alone. I know how much you like helping people, but this isn't the case for you."

"So everyone tells me," I said. "Why are you involved, but not Edie's parents?"

Hattie's face went somber, and she quickly glanced over her shoulder, as if to make sure Edie wasn't sneaking up behind us. "Edie's parents are both dead," she breathed into my ear. "Her mother died of cancer, and then a couple of years later, her father had a heart attack."

"Oh my goodness, I'm so sorry," I said, pressing my hand against my chest as I pictured Edie at Hattie's table, so small and fragile despite her large stomach.

Hattie nodded sadly. "It was such a tragedy. Edie was in high school at the time. Her father had started drinking after her mother's death, and a lot of people thought the alcohol contributed to his heart attack. As you can imagine, that baby means everything to her."

"I can imagine."

"My house was on her rotation," Hattie said as she opened the hall closet door, revealing two winter coats—one of which was mine. I ignored them.

"Rotation?"

"She was only sixteen when her father died, so we had to make sure she wasn't going into the system," Hattie said matter-of-factly. I assumed "system" was synonymous with foster care. "She would rotate through my house and a few others. I would get her approximately one week a month."

I wondered how they could make that work legally. I couldn't imagine the state of Wisconsin allowing a teenager to just rotate through neighbors' houses. Then again, this community seemed more than capable of expertly avoiding legal scrutiny. "Is this common practice for the 1888ers?"

She gave me a look as she thrust my coat into my arms. "Do you really think I'm going to tell you that?"

"Where's the coat you're giving Edie?" I asked.

"It's right there," she pointed to the other coat.

"But what are you going to wear?"

She waved her hand. "I'll be fine. Don't worry about me. I never leave the house anyway."

Oh no. This wouldn't do at all. I handed her back my coat. "Take it."

Her eyes widened, and she stepped back. "No, that's yours. I couldn't do that."

"Yes, you can. It's January. You both need a winter coat."

She shook her head violently, refusing to take it. "That's your good winter coat. I won't take it."

Ugh. I looked around before plucking my second coat off the rack and gave it to Hattie. "Here. And I'm not taking no for an answer."

After a bit of back and forth, Hattie finally accepted my second-best winter coat. I could see the gratitude in her eyes, but I couldn't help feeling slightly ashamed as I put on my coat. I was leaving an old, sick woman and a pregnant girl alone in a cold house, and all I was worried about was getting my coat back.

"Is there anything else I can help you with?" I asked Hattie. "Like maybe buy you some groceries?"

She waved her hand again. "We're fine. You've already done so much. You saved Edie's life!"

"Again, I did what anyone would do," I said. "What about your heat?"

She gave me a funny look. "My heat?"

"Yes, is your furnace working properly? Or maybe you need a little extra for the gas company?"

Her confusion deepened. "My furnace is fine and I'm up to date on my bills. Why are you asking?"

I thought of the chill in the kitchen … the icy touch that trailed down my spine when they first talked about The Forgotten.

It was probably a draft, I told myself.

Hattie was still staring at me, a concerned look in her eyes. I forced a smile onto my face. *It's just a draft.* "No reason."

***

Needless to say, and despite what Hattie and Edie wanted, I had no intention of dropping the investigation.

If anything, I was even more committed than before. The fact that those two women were sitting in Hattie's house without any protection (other than the notion that "the 1888ers will save us") was incredible to me. What if whoever burned down 88 Spirits decided to do the same to Hattie's house? How would they be able to stop it, much less get out in time, especially if the arsonist blocked the doors again? I couldn't imagine either of them climbing through a window.

As far as I could see, the only way to protect Hattie and Edie, and maybe others as well, was to find out who was behind the arson, which I fully intended to do.

The only thing I was missing was a plan.

Clearly, the first thing I needed to do was figure out the identity of The Forgotten. But how? I didn't know any other 1888ers, other than Carol, who wasn't exactly an 1888er. I suspected neither Pat nor Wyle would be open to talking to me about it, although, to be fair, I wasn't sure if Wyle would know any Forgottens either. That left Mildred … the wild card.

I decided to start with Carol.

The moment I got home, I called her. I would have preferred to stop by her house, but I didn't know her address, and she had specifically told me to call her with updates.

She answered on the first ring, almost as if she had been sitting right next to it, waiting to pounce. "Hello?"

"Hi, is this Carol?"

"Charlie, is that you?" There was something in her tone that I couldn't read. It sounded almost frantic, like desperation, but there was also grief.

I wondered if I'd interrupted her right when she was about to have a good old- fashioned cry.

"I can call back if this isn't a good time."

"No, no." There was the sound of nose-blowing. "This is important. Do you have something to report?"

I cringed. A part of me wanted to remind her that no, I hadn't sent her an invoice, and I had no intention of doing so, so no I wasn't going to be giving her "regular reports," but again I decided arguing about this arrangement wasn't worth our time. "I might. Have you heard about The Forgotten?"

Silence. I couldn't even hear her breathing.

"Carol? Are you there?"

"I'm here." Her voice was abrupt. "Who told you about The Forgotten? Was it Edie? Did you find her?"

Oh geez. This was yet another reason I had no intention of getting paid for investigating. I wasn't about to tell anyone where Edie was—at least not until I had a much better idea of where the danger was coming from. "How am I supposed to find her when no one will talk to me?"

"Well how do you know about The Forgotten then?"

"It's not just 1888ers who know about The Forgotten," I said, even though I had absolutely no idea if that were true or not. But I assumed there had to be at least one person, someone like Mildred, who would know about The Forgotten.

"Are you saying they had something to do with the fire?" There was real fear in her voice.

"I don't know, but I think it's worth asking a few questions. Apparently, your husband had to kick them out of 88 Spirits a few times recently. Did he say anything to you about it?"

"No, but … oh no." There was a muffled sound, like she was covering the mouthpiece, although I wasn't sure why. Was someone there with her? After a moment, she was back. "Charlie, you've got to get to the bottom of this, and fast."

"Well, I'd like to, but I need a little more to go on …"

"No!" Now, the edge in her voice was bordering on hysteria. "Listen to me. You have to figure this out. I can't sell this house if people think The Forgotten were involved in my husband's murder, and I need to get out of here!"

"I understand," I said, but I didn't. At least, not completely. What was it about The Forgotten that instilled so much fear in people? It couldn't just be that they were dabbling in some sort of black magic stuff, could it? "But in order to do that, I need some direction."

"You have direction," she snapped. "I already told you about my husband borrowing money from loan sharks, and now, there's evidence he was dealing with The Forgotten. There's the missing piece."

"My understanding is The Forgotten aren't loan sharks …"

"That doesn't mean they aren't used by the loan sharks," she interrupted. "My goodness, think! What am I hiring you for?"

"Well, you haven't hired me at all actually," I said. I was about to add that at this point, I wasn't interested in doing any further work for her if this was going to be her attitude, but I knew that would be a lie.

She took a deep, shuddering breath. "I'm sorry. I shouldn't have snapped at you. I'm just … I'm just so overwhelmed. Arthur is gone, and now I have to worry not just about these loan sharks, but about The Forgotten coming after me? I don't even know what to do. All I know is that I have to get out of here, and the sooner the better. Will you help me?"

My earlier irritation almost instantly evaporated. Carol was going through a lot, and everyone dealt with grief differently. "I'm trying to," I said, softening my voice. "But to do that, I need more help. Do you know who any of The Forgotten are?"

"They're a secretive group who keep a low profile," Carol said, which wasn't exactly an answer. "Probably the best thing you can do is ask whoever told you about The Forgotten for help. Even if they don't give you a name of an actual Forgotten, they might know someone who knows someone who knows someone … you know."

I pictured myself showing up at Hattie's door to ask more questions. Along with doubting I would get anywhere, as neither of them seemed open to telling me any more than they already had, I was also leery of doing anything that would make them the center of attention. I had already visited Hattie twice in a week, which was twice as much as typical. Going back a third time felt like pushing it.

But before I could open my mouth to ask her if she "knew someone who might know someone," she was telling me she had to go and abruptly hanging up.

Great. Now what? My choices had apparently dwindled to asking Pat, Wyle, or Mildred.

None of them were great.

The only other thing I could think about doing was going to each of my tea customers, or, really, anyone with whom I was friendly with, and asking them for a lead.

Also not ideal.

For lack of something better to do, I made my way into the kitchen to make some tea. I was a firm believer that a cup of tea could cure just about everything, and I was about to put that theory to the test.

I had just filled the teakettle and put it on the stove when the doorbell rang. Could I have possibly lucked out and had a new lead randomly show up on my doorstep?

If it were, I would never doubt the power of tea again.

I headed for the door.

Chapter 11

Pat was standing on my front porch, holding a wiggling Tiki. "Do you have a moment?"

"Of course," I said as alarm bells started going off in my head. Pat was never so formal. Usually, she'd just barrel in the moment I opened the door. Sometimes, she let herself in, not even waiting for me to come to the door.

I backed up as she stepped through the entrance and placed Tiki on the ground, who immediately ran to greet me. She wore a dapper red and black diamond sweater with red ribbons by her ears. Pat, however, wore an oversized plain, gray sweatshirt sporting a brown stain. The stain was less off-putting than the fact that I knew she had a matching red and black diamond sweater, and she almost always matched Tiki.

Something was not right.

"Would you like a cup of tea? I was in the middle of making a pot," I asked.

She nodded, pushing her hair out of her face. It seemed greasier and flatter than normal. The alarm bells started ringing louder.

I led the way into the kitchen, where I finished making the tea and set out a plate of cookies next to a plate of homemade dog biscuits. Pat played with her tea mug, but didn't drink nor take a cookie, which was also very unlike her.

I picked up my own mug, trying to tamp down the alarm bells that had turned into sirens. "What's up?" I hoped my voice didn't sound as panicked as I felt.

She let out a sigh. "I owe you an explanation. Well …" she paused and rolled her eyes. "Richard thinks I owe you an explanation. And, while normally I wouldn't say this, I think he's probably right." Her eyes flickered up toward me. "Just to be clear, it's not that I mind you knowing this. I just hate talking about it. *Hate*."

She grimaced and reached out and broke off a piece of cookie, but instead of eating it, she gave it to a very excited Tiki. I wisely kept my mouth shut, even though there were healthy and delicious doggy treats sitting right next to the cookies. A few cookies wouldn't hurt Tiki.

"Growing up, I had a best friend named Patty. We would jokingly call ourselves twins, even though we looked nothing alike. She was tall and thin with blonde hair and blue eyes. Anyway." She reached out to break off another piece of cookie for Tiki. "When we were seniors in high school, she fell in love with an 1888er. His name was Rex, and he was a few years older than us." She sighed again, shaking her head in near despair.

"Everyone told her it was a dreadful idea, getting involved with an 1888er, but she didn't care. She was sure their love would transcend any issues they might have. In fact, she thought it might even transcend the curse itself. Love conquers all, and all that nonsense. But of course, she was young and didn't listen."

She paused, breaking off another piece of cookie for Tiki, a faraway expression in her eyes. "It happened in June on a Saturday night. Her car went off the road and hit a tree. By the time anyone found her, she was dead."

"Oh no," I gasped, pressing my hand to my mouth. "I'm so sorry. That must have been terrible for you."

"It was," she said, her voice quiet. "Especially since it made no sense. She was found on County Road FFF going out of town at around four in the morning by a construction worker. But what possible reason would she have to be out there in the middle of the night? It was nowhere near either her parent's house or where Rex lived. According to Rex, they had gone out to eat and then back to his place to watch some television before she left around eleven. But the coroner estimated that her death probably occurred between midnight and two a.m. So what was she doing for over an hour before the accident? Rex claimed everything was normal when she left. They hadn't been fighting, nor had she been drinking. But why was she out there?"

"How did the cops explain it?

Pat snorted. "They didn't. After a few days of poking around and asking the public if they happened to be driving down that road any time after eleven that night, they pretty much decided it was an accident. Most likely, a deer had been in the road, and Patty swerved to avoid hitting it. She lost control and hit a tree."

That seemed plausible. Deer were everywhere around us, and hitting (or almost hitting) them was pretty common. But that didn't explain the time inconsistencies.

"What do you think happened?" I asked.

Pat's shoulders slumped. "I don't know. I still don't know. At the time, I was sure Rex was involved, but now …" she shook her head and gazed out the kitchen window. "My dad had a friend who was a cop. Once it became clear that the investigation wasn't going anywhere, I went to see him. I told him my concerns, and he agreed it looked a little fishy. He promised to look into it. After a day or so, he called to tell me that there WERE inconsistencies with her death. The coroner had initially ruled that the accident hadn't immediately killed her … that she had …" Pat swallowed hard. "Well, it had taken a bit for her to die from her injuries. But the coroner had also found some bruising that wasn't compatible with the accident. And there was something odd about the toxicology report, so they were running more tests. But he didn't elaborate on what was odd, or what tests they were doing.

"By that point, I was even more convinced that Rex had something to do with it. So that weekend, I marched over to his place. He lived in a tiny apartment above a garage. A real dump. Patty had pointed it out to me once. Middle of summer, no air conditioning … I couldn't figure out why she would ever go over there." She paused to take another deep, unsteady breath. "Even though it was in the afternoon, Rex had been drinking, which should have been an immediate sign to leave. But again, I was young, grieving, and just not thinking straight in general."

"It didn't go well?" I asked, although based on her expression, that seemed pretty obvious.

She rolled her eyes. "That's an understatement. I immediately started yelling at Rex, accusing him of killing Patty. Of course he denied it, so I started telling him what my dad's friend found out."

Her eyes glazed over, as if she were back in front of that shabby apartment, the oppressive heat and humidity adding fuel to the fire. "I still remember how his face turned white after I told him about the unexplained bruises. 'You need to leave right now,' he said. Of course, I refused, so he smashed the beer bottle he was holding on the side of the door and threatened me with the broken end, telling me to leave and never come back."

"Did he hurt you?" I asked.

Pat shook her head. "No, but he did get me to leave, which, in retrospect, was a good thing."

"Well, yeah, I would agree with that," I said.

Pat gave me a steady look. "You haven't heard the rest yet."

I shifted uneasily in my chair, starting to get a bad feeling about where this was going. "So what happened?"

"I went to the police station to find my dad's friend. He wasn't working that day, so I went to his house."

My eyes widened. "You went to his home?"

She shrugged. "I was on a mission. I was sure Rex was guilty, and I wasn't sure if I could trust anyone at the Redemption Police Department. I found him puttering around his backyard with his gardening tools. I was a mess by then, practically shaking with rage and righteousness. I told him what happened and how I was sure it was Rex. I expected him to agree with me, maybe race inside to put his uniform on, so he could go arrest Rex. But that wasn't at all what happened."

She looked up at me, her expression a strange mixture of grief, disgust, and the faintest touch of that long-ago rage. "He looked at me with this sad, patronizing expression on his face, and I just knew …" Her fists tightened. "I knew at that moment they got to him."

"Who got to him?"

"Whoever is in charge of the police," she said grimly. "He told me he was going to call me on Monday to let me know, but as it turned out, the coroner was mistaken. Those bruises were part of his initial review, but after a closer examination, they were probably caused by the accident."

My jaw dropped. "Really?" Although maybe I shouldn't be surprised, considering everyone's reaction to the police investigating the fire.

"Really. So, I asked about the toxicology report, and he said that also was nothing. I was seething, and I think he knew it. He told me how sorry he was about my friend's death, but that I needed to accept that it was an accident and stop running around town investigating or accusing people of murder. He was very clear I should stay away from Rex."

Her lips turned up in a smile that didn't have a lot of humor in it. "Fat chance that was going to happen. But the joke was on me. As soon as I left, he called my dad to tell him what was going on. Of course, my parents responded by grounding me for three weeks. I was beside myself, but again, in retrospect, it was a good thing."

She paused again, looking toward the window. She looked as if she had aged ten years just sitting at my table. "About two weeks into my grounding, I got word that Rex was dead."

I almost fell out of my chair. "*What?*"

She gave me a knowing look. "I know, right?"

"How did *he* die?"

"Freak construction accident. I don't even remember what happened. I do remember there were a lot of witnesses, and it seemed pretty clear it was an accident."

"Wow, that's … wow." I didn't even know what to say.

Pat met my eyes. "I know."

There was a long moment of silence. I thought about Rex, first losing his girlfriend and then dying in a freak construction accident. Did it happen because he was still mourning his girlfriend and not paying close enough attention? Or maybe he did have something to do with her death after all, and it was guilt that caused the accident?

"What did you do?" I asked.

Pat shrugged. "I stopped investigating, for one. I didn't know what to think. I still couldn't believe that Rex didn't have something to do with her death, but to have him die, too, also in a freak accident …" She leaned forward across the table, causing Tiki to let out a little yip as she nearly smothered the little dog with her ample chest. "You see what was going on, right?"

"Um …" I wasn't sure where she was going.

She gave me a look as if it should have been obvious. "It's the curse!"

"Well, we don't know that," I said. "It's possible someone killed Patty, just like you originally thought, but it wasn't Rex. Maybe Rex knew who it was and confronted him, and that's why he ended up in a …"

Pat was shaking her head. "No, you're not getting it. Even if it WAS murder, and it's possible either or both were murdered, it's still the curse. You don't get murdered if you aren't cursed."

"Well …" I didn't think that was necessarily true, but before I could answer, Pat kept going.

"Okay, look." She flattened her hands on the table as she leaned forward, her eyes intense, prompting another squeak from Tiki. That is, until she realized there was a piece of chocolate chip cookie near her that she could gobble up. "I know most people who are murdered aren't necessarily cursed. But to have something like this happen? Something this freaky? That's what I'm talking about. The 1888ers *are* cursed, and anyone who is in contact with them for any length of time is also at risk of being cursed."

Her voice was so firm, so decisive, I knew there was no way I was going to be able to convince her of anything different. "It does seem like a lot of bad luck," I said lamely.

She rolled her eyes. "Not bad luck. Charlie, look. I get it. You're not a believer. But …" her voice suddenly and unexpectedly broke. "I can't lose someone else I love to the 1888er curse. I just can't. I know you don't believe, but that doesn't mean you're immune. Patty didn't believe either, and look what happened to her." Her voice was thick with emotion, and she swallowed hard. "Please, for my sake, don't investigate this. Don't get involved. Just leave it alone."

I reached across the table to grab her hands. They were ice cold. "I hear you. I do. But I can't stop thinking about the innocent people who may be in danger, like Edie. You keep saying the police won't help. So who will?"

Pat's face hardened. "The 1888ers will take care of themselves. They always do."

What was going on in this town? How was it that Pat sounded just like Edie and Hattie? "But Edie is pregnant …" I started to say, but Pat interrupted me.

"Edie will be fine. Don't worry."

"How do you know?"

"Because I do." Pat's face had flattened, but there was a softness in her eyes. "Charlie, I know how much you want to help people. And nine times out of ten, your help is really needed. But not here. At best, you're just going to get in the way and waste a bunch of time, and at worst, you'll get someone hurt or killed. You might even get yourself hurt or killed. Can you please, for my sake, leave this one alone?"

I stared at Pat, into her eyes pleading with me, her voice cracking with emotion. I didn't want to bring her any more pain. And I could see how much she still struggled with her friend's death, even though I didn't believe in curses.

My mind instantly went back to my dream. Surrounded by fire, the smell of smoke in my nostrils, the words that almost sounded like a curse.

I pushed it away. It was just a dream … nothing to do with reality. Reality was Pat still grieving over her friend, and her worrying about me because she couldn't help but see parallels between myself and her friend.

Did I really want to make things worse for her?

But then I thought about Hattie and Edie, and how frail they looked sitting at that broken kitchen table. Yes, they told me they would be fine—that the 1888ers would protect them. But would they? Arthur might have thought exactly the same—that he too would be safe—and look what happened to him. And even though I'd never seen the man, I assumed he was better able to take care of himself than either Hattie or Edie.

And then there was Carol. While I had no intention of letting her hire me, I had told her I was going to investigate. Was I ready to go back on my word?

On the other hand, it really did seem like no one, other than Carol, wanted me to look into the case. Not even Mildred and Tilde thought it was a good idea. Maybe it was best to listen to everyone and just let it go.

Even if it had gotten under my skin.

But I couldn't just leave Hattie and Edie defenseless.

Maybe there was a way I could do both.

"I can do that," I said.

Pat briefly closed her eyes in relief before reaching for a cookie. "That calls for a celebration," she said, holding it up. Tiki looked up expectantly as she licked her chops. "Not for you," she said fondly as she selected a doggy treat for Tiki. I smiled as I topped off her tea, which I was sure had gone cold, glad to see that she was feeling well enough to get the cookies and treats correctly doled out.

And once she left, I could wrap up the final loose ends of the case.

Chapter 12

I had every intention of letting it go.

I told Pat I could, and I intended to.

After I told Wyle what I'd learned.

As I approached the front doors of the Redemption Police Department, I couldn't help but notice the dirty snow piled high along the sidewalks. As the cold wind whistled past my cheeks and rattled the bare trees that flanked the front of the station, I knew I was doing something that no one wanted. No one wanted the police involved. Not Edie, not Hattie, not Carol.

But what else was I supposed to do? There were clear signs that someone had deliberately set 88 Spirits on fire, and that fire had killed Arthur and almost killed Edie. It was very possible that whoever was behind it might try again. Carol was worried for her life, and Edie and Hattie really ought to be. There was no way I could live with myself if any of them ended up hurt or dead because I didn't tell the cops.

Besides, Wyle wasn't exactly "the cops." I mean, he was, but he was one of the good ones. He wanted to investigate this case. If anyone could get to the bottom of this absolute mess, I was confident it would be Wyle.

I pulled open the door and stepped into the overheated and nearly empty lobby. A young woman with her jacket unzipped was huddled up in one of the black plastic chairs that lined the wall, a baby in a car carrier in the chair next to her. Her brown, noticeably unwashed hair was pulled up in a messy ponytail, and she was peering at something on a clipboard with exhausted eyes.

An officer was filling out paperwork behind a glass partition. I stepped up to ask to see Wyle, but then I saw him standing near the back. He was talking to an older, bearded officer with glasses and a round gut. He immediately spotted me and quickly waved before wrapping up his conversation and heading toward me.

"Can I help you?" The officer filling out paperwork was staring at me. His voice was nasally, as if he had a bad cold, and I could see both his eyes and nose were red.

"I've got this, Pete, thanks," Wyle said, opening the gate to let me in. "What's up?" The light tone of his voice was at odds with the intensity of his stare.

"I have some info on the fire," I said, keeping my words intentionally vague and low, as I figured he would know what I was talking about. "Do you have a moment?"

It was so subtle, I almost missed it—his eyes widening slightly as he quickly glanced around before rearranging his features back into a neutral expression. "I do. Let's go talk."

I assumed he was going to lead me to his messy desk, which was always overflowing with towers of paper and files that I was sure would tip over at any second. I was preparing myself for the stench of burned coffee and nervous sweat, but instead, he led me to the back where the interrogation rooms were and gestured for me to enter.

"Why are we talking here?" I asked as I sat in one of the uncomfortable folding chairs next to a flimsy wooden table.

"Well, you always complain about my desk. I figured here, you wouldn't have to look at it." He flashed me a small smile, one that didn't reach his eyes, as he sat down in front of me.

I decided not to push it. Especially since, truth be told, I was glad for the privacy. I didn't have to worry about who was listening in.

He folded his arms and leaned against the table. I noticed he didn't have his usual notebook and pen, which he pretty much always had when I stopped by in the past to share what I'd uncovered. "So, what have you dug up? I know you've been investigating despite the fact everyone told you not to." The look he shot me was only faintly exasperated.

"You say it like getting involved was my plan all along," I said.

He rolled his eyes. "Of course it wasn't. It's never your intention, yet somehow, you always get involved." His tone was faintly affectionate, which made my insides twist in an unexpected way.

"This is different," I insisted. "Honestly, this wasn't my intention."

His lips quirked into a smile again, this one seeming a bit more genuine. "Uh huh. Whatever. So, what did you uncover, wholly accidentally of course, this time?"

Ugh. He could be so insufferable. "Okay, look. I'll tell you what I know, but first, you have to promise me something."

He shot me a wary look. "What sort of promise?"

"That you don't go talk to anyone. Or, if you do, you don't let on what I've told you."

He gave me another exasperated look. "Charlie, you know I can't do that."

I pressed my hands against the table. "But you have to. No one wants anything to do with the Redemption police, and if they know I'm talking to you, they'll never trust me again." Even as I said the words, I wondered why I cared. Wasn't my plan to stop investigating after I told Wyle everything I knew?

Well, yes, but I also don't want to burn any bridges, I told myself. Hattie was still a tea customer, and I didn't want to destroy that relationship.

Yes, but Edie and Carol are not tea customers and likely never will be, a little voice inside me said. I decided to ignore it.

Wyle didn't answer right away. Instead, he gave me a long, unreadable look. "I'll do my best," he finally said.

That wasn't exactly what I wanted, but I figured it was as good as I was going to get. "Have you heard of The Forgotten?"

Something flickered in his eyes, but it disappeared so fast that I wasn't sure if I had imagined it or not. "The Forgotten?"

"It's apparently some sort of 1888er subgroup," I said. "Unlike most 1888ers, who have just accepted that they're cursed, The Forgotten are actively trying to fight against it."

Wyle turned away, his eyes unfocused. "I think I've heard something, but …"

"What?" I asked quickly, perhaps too quickly.

He shook his head. "It's nothing, at least nothing helpful. What about The Forgotten?"

"It's possible they're behind the arson."

Wyle's gaze sharpened. "How do you know?"

I briefly summarized what Edie had told me about what she had overheard.

Wyle's nostrils flared. "You found Edie." It wasn't a question. "Where is she?"

"I can't tell you that," I said.

He glared at me. "You're withholding evidence in an active police investigation."

I raised an eyebrow. "Am I?"

There was a dangerous silence as he stared at me. I knew I was playing with fire.

And I couldn't help but wonder again why we were tucked back in an interrogation room and why he didn't have his notebook. The whole case stunk to high heaven, and I couldn't wait to hand it over to Wyle and be done with it.

Assuming that was even an option. In my head, I kept replaying Mildred, Tilde, and Pat's laughter at the idea of the police investigating.

"Charlie." His voice had deepened. "You need to trust me."

"I do trust you," I said. "Why do you think I'm here? But I also know you can't promise not to go talk to Edie, and right now, that could be bad for her." The last thing I wanted was Wyle showing up at Hattie's doorstep, especially so soon after I had been there.

He sighed. "Fine. For now, at least."

I almost fell out of my chair. I didn't expect him to capitulate so quickly.

"Are you at least going to tell me who these Forgotten are?" he asked.

"I was hoping you might know that," I said. "Unfortunately, I don't have a clue."

He winced as he rubbed the back of his neck. "Great. Anything else?"

"Actually, yes. It's also possible Arthur was involved with some shady organizations."

His eyes widened. "Really? Like what?"

I filled him in on the possibility of Arthur having borrowed money from a loan shark. I could see his fingers twitch several times as he listened to me, as if he really wanted to be taking notes.

"You think maybe The Forgotten loaned him money?" he asked when I was done.

"That was my first thought, but I was told The Forgotten don't have much money. Of course, that doesn't mean what I was told is correct," I said.

Wyle nodded again, his eyes unfocused. His fingers twitched again.

"Where's your notebook?" I asked.

His face snapped toward me, and he blinked a couple of times before answering. "Oh. Silly me, I forgot." He spread his hands out and gave me a self-conscious grin, but there was something off about it.

I didn't bother to point out the notebook and pen in his pocket. I could see it from where I sat across from him. More to the point, he also knew it was there, because more than once, his hand drifted toward that pocket before settling back on the table.

Yes, there was definitely something fishy going on.

"How IS the case going?" I asked, tilting my head and smiling. "Anything you can share?" This was standard with us—sharing what we could with each other.

"It's going," Wyle said, but his eyes had shifted to a spot behind me. "At least, that's my understanding. It's not my case, so I don't have the latest info."

Fair enough. The Redemption police force was small, but not so small that Wyle would automatically be involved in every single investigation.

But that didn't mean there wasn't something off.

"I'll keep you posted," Wyle said, getting up while still avoiding my eyes. "I don't suppose this means you're done investigating and you'll finally leave it to the professionals?" There was a strange, hopeful note in his voice. Normally, I would assume he was hopeful that I would stop investigating. But this time, I got the strong impression he was hopeful I would keep going.

"You're in luck," I said. "Now that I've told you everything important, I have every intention of being done with this case."

Was that disappointment on his face? "Good," he said, but his mouth had flattened, and he sounded anything but happy. "I'm glad you're finally coming around to the right side."

"Don't get too excited," I said lightly. "Just because I'm no longer investigating *this* case doesn't mean I won't be investigating others."

He mock-staggered, pressing his hand to his heart. "And just like that, you're back. I should have known it couldn't last."

I jokingly punched his arm, but even our teasing seemed forced and unnatural. Whatever it was about the 1888ers and this case, I was glad to be done with it.

Chapter 13

I was in the kitchen making a big batch of my lemon-lavender tea when the phone rang.

Since handing over the investigation to Wyle two days ago, I had gotten a ton of things done. First, I had cleaned my house from top to bottom and done a massive amount of laundry. Then, I got caught up on all my tea orders, and now, I was working ahead. One of the downsides of investigating was that it kept me from staying on top of my tea orders and household chores, but all of that had now been rectified. As soon as I finished the batch of tea, I was going grocery shopping, so I could create a bunch of casseroles and soup that I'd then freeze for days when I was in the middle of a case.

I was glad I had the time to get myself organized and cross off the to-dos from my list. Why would I want to waste my precious time investigating a case that no one wanted my help with anyway? This was so much better.

I repeated this to myself often as I worked, reminding myself I was relieved to have the case off my shoulders. Never mind that my mind kept picturing Hattie and Edie sitting at that crooked kitchen table, looking so small and frail. Never mind that I kept seeing the fear in Carol's eyes when she told me she was scared that whoever lent Arthur money was going to come after her.

None of that was my problem. Hattie and Edie didn't want my help, and Carol … well, she refused to give me anything to work with. If she had provided me with even a single name of someone to talk to who might know who The Forgotten were, I could have done something. But she didn't, and I had run out of options.

It was better this way.

I wiped my hands with a dish towel and went to answer the phone. It was probably one of my tea clients calling me back. I had phoned several of them to tell them I could drop off their orders before grocery shopping, if that worked for them.

"Oh good, you're home." It was Wyle. "We have a problem."

Frowning, I tucked the receiver between my shoulder and neck so I could return to my tea-making, just as I normally would. There was nothing to worry about, especially not that uneasy feeling that had started to unfurl itself in my stomach again. "What do you mean? And where are you?" It sounded like he was outside, as I could hear the sounds of traffic behind him.

"I'm at a pay phone at … well, that doesn't matter. Look, I don't have much time, and I hate to ask, but I need your help."

Oh no. That uneasy feeling was starting to wind its way up my spine. "What do you mean?"

"You're going to need to keep investigating the arson."

I almost dropped the phone. "*What?*"

"I know, I know. I wouldn't ask, but my hands are tied."

Oh man. "What happened to leaving investigations to the professionals?"

He let out a mirthless bark of laughter. "Well, when the professionals are barred from investigating, it's kind of hard to leave it to them."

My stomach seemed to hit the floor. "What are you talking about? Are you okay?"

"I've been demoted."

"*What?*" This was worse than I'd expected. "You were actually demoted?"

"Not officially. Not yet, anyway." He sucked in a breath. "I'm on traffic duty. They said it's temporary, as they're apparently short on help or something. A couple of guys are out. It's not unusual to have to step in when we're short- handed, but let's just say the timing is a little suspect."

I closed my eyes. "Don't tell me. You were asking questions about The Forgotten."

"Well, that and just general questions about how the case is going. I hate to say it, but it sure seems Pat and the other ladies were right."

Oh man … speaking of Pat, she was going to kill me if I got involved again. "What can I do?"

"What you normally do." There was an urgency in his voice. "Investigate. Find me something solid to work with. I need evidence, proof, something that is irrefutable that I can take to my boss and force them to open the case."

My hand tightened on the receiver. "Seriously?"

"You know I wouldn't ask if there were any other options. It has to come from someone else, like you. If it comes from me, even if I'm investigating on my own time, I'm going to get written up."

My eyes widened. "They said that."

"In so many words. So what do you think? Can you do it?"

I was silent for a moment. On one hand, I had promised Pat. Well, I sort of promised her. I told her I could leave it alone, and I did leave it alone. For a couple of days anyway. Hattie and Edie also told me to let it go. And on top of that, I had no leads.

But on the other hand … again, a picture of Hattie and Edie filled my mind. Not to mention all the questions surrounding what had really happened at that bar.

"I'll do it," I said, mentally apologizing to Pat.

Wyle let out a breath. I couldn't tell if he was relieved or wondering if he had lost his mind. I was certainly wondering if I had lost mine. "Keep me informed every step of the way," he said. "I want to know what you're up to. No Lone Ranger stuff. Got it?"

"Got it."

"Charlie, I'm serious." His voice had deepened. "I don't know what's going on, but you need to be careful. Promise me you won't do anything stupid."

What, like investigate a case that no one wants to be investigated, including the person who was trapped in a burning bar? I bit my tongue to keep myself from saying it out loud, because all it would do was upset him, and it wasn't his fault that he was in this situation. And I hadn't told him about Pat, so for all he knew, I was still investigating even if I told him I wasn't. "I'll do my best."

He muttered something under his breath that sounded like a curse. "Great. I'm already regretting this."

****

I settled into my corner table at the Brew House, a latte in front of me, but I was too nervous to drink it. I kept telling myself I had nothing to be nervous about, as there was nothing wrong with meeting a friend for coffee. But I was having trouble convincing myself.

Especially since normally, I would go to Aunt May's Diner for a coffee meet up. Not that there was anything wrong with the Brew House; in fact, you could argue the coffee was better than Aunt May's. There were certainly no lattes on the menu at the diner. Nevertheless, Aunt May's was my go-to, not the Brew House. The Brew House catered more to tourists and professionals ducking in for a quick coffee break before heading back to work. Aunt May's was more for the locals, which was precisely why I wasn't there. The last thing I wanted was for Pat to see me … or for someone to tell Pat they'd seen me.

Which led me to my second point. Normally, if I were meeting a friend, that friend would be Pat. If it wasn't Pat, Pat would have been invited. I certainly wouldn't be sneaking around at the Brew House meeting Mildred like I was doing something wrong. Because I wasn't doing anything wrong.

But no matter how much I repeated that to myself, I couldn't squash down the guilt that filled me like a noxious gas.

She'll understand, I told myself, even if I wasn't sure I believed it. *Once she knows the full story, she'll understand. Pat wouldn't want anything to happen to Hattie, Edie, or the baby.*

True, but she also didn't want anything to happen to me. Not to mention that I DID tell her I was letting it go.

Hence why I was hiding at the Brew House waiting for Mildred. Because maybe the best way to handle Pat was to make sure she never knew. A "What you don't know can't hurt you" sort of thing.

I didn't think it would be too difficult. I'd spend a day or two poking around, find a couple of solid leads for Wyle, and boom. I'd walk away, and Pat would be none the wiser.

Piece of cake.

I picked up my latte to see if it had cooled off and nearly dropped it into my lap. Was that … Mildred?

Oh dear heaven.

Mildred stalked into the coffee shop looking like some sort of spy. She was dressed in all black, with a black fedora, of all things, topping off the ensemble along with huge black sunglasses. She hunched her shoulders and quickly skirted around the lobby as if she were expecting a criminal to pop up from behind the coffee counter.

"Mildred! Fancy seeing you here." One of the women who had been waiting for her coffee order sang out.

"Oh." Mildred seemed a little flustered. "I'm just meeting someone." She waved a black-gloved hand toward me. The woman peered over her shoulder, adjusting her glasses to get a better look at me.

I wanted to crawl under the table.

In retrospect, I probably shouldn't have mentioned to Mildred that the reason I didn't want to meet her at either Aunt May's or The Redemption Detective Agency's office was because I wanted to keep this meeting under wraps. "The fewer people who know, the better," I had told her.

Mildred's agreement was far too enthusiastic. I should have known something was up.

"I can't believe Helen recognized me," Mildred said, sliding into the chair in front of me, cup of coffee in hand. "I knew I should have worn the wig."

A wig? Could this get any worse?

"And maybe the eyepatch," she mused.

"Okay," I said quickly. Clearly, it could get worse, and I didn't need to hear anymore. "Thanks for meeting me on such short notice."

"Of course," Mildred said, removing her sunglasses and replacing them with her regular glasses. "I'm always available to help you with any of your cases. That's what friends are for!"

"I appreciate that," I said, and while I did, the jury was still out as to whether I was going to regret this or not. "So, as I told you, this is a little … sensitive. That's why I need you to keep all of this to yourself."

"My lips are sealed," Mildred said while pantomiming turning a key to lock her lips.

I could only hope. "Will this be an issue between you and Tilde?"

Mildred waved her hand. "Don't worry about Tilde. I'll handle her."

Man, I hoped that was true. All that kept flashing through my head was the Mildred who used to sit in her house and report on her neighbors. Although maybe now that she had a job (I used the word "job" loosely, as Emily, Tilde's niece and the office manager of The Redemption Detective Agency, had informed me no one was getting paid at the agency), she wouldn't feel the need to share everything. Or, even if she did still feel the need, she could control it.

Hopefully.

Man, I was living a lot in Hope World. But what other options did I have? Who else did I know who could possibly point me in the direction of the identity of The Forgotten?

No one. If Mildred couldn't help me, I wasn't sure what I was going to do. Start asking my friends one by one and hope they didn't mention anything to Pat? Ugh. This was turning into such a mess.

Mildred reached for the sugar packets and started doctoring her coffee. "So, how can I help?"

I took a deep breath. "What do you know about The Forgotten?"

Mildred's hand stilled. She looked up at me, her pale-blue eyes wide. "Oh, Charlie. You don't want to know about them."

"That may be so, but I don't have much of a choice."

Mildred was already shaking her head, and I could feel my stomach slowly sink to the floor. What if she refused to help me? "Trust me, you don't want anything to do with them."

"And I'm not going to do anything with them. I just need to know who they are."

She stopped shaking her head and peered at me over her glasses. "Why? Does this have something to do with 88 Spirits?"

I gritted my teeth. I had really been hoping I could get the information I needed without giving much to Mildred. "Well, if it's as dangerous as you say, the less I tell you, the better."

She clucked her tongue. "I'm not worried for myself. I'm an old woman. They're not going to hurt me."

Tiny alarm bells started going off in my head. "Is that what they do? Hurt people?"

"That's the rumor, but I don't know how true it is. There's a lot of stuff said about The Forgotten. Most of it is probably nonsense."

"Like what?"

Mildred glanced around the coffee shop, perhaps to see if anyone was listening, but there was only one other person in the dining area, a young man with a beret who was busy scribbling in his notebook. He was also far enough away that I didn't think he would hear us. Luckily, Mildred's friend had already left. "That they're a bunch of hoodlums causing trouble. Drugs, gambling, vandalism, stealing, that sort of thing."

I felt myself grow cold. "Money laundering?"

Mildred sniffed. "I doubt it. Not that they wouldn't want to get into money laundering. I'm sure they would if they could, but I don't think any of them think that far ahead."

"So you know who they are then?"

"I know the type," Mildred said.

My shoulders slumped. "But not specific names?"

"They're very secretive," Mildred said.

"So I've heard." As frustrated as I was with the walls I kept hitting, I had to hand it to The Forgotten. They seemed to have been able to crack something that had so far eluded me—keeping the rest of the town out of their business.

Mildred cocked her head, a knowing look on her face, as though she knew what I was thinking. "Honestly, Charlie. No one wants anything to do with The Forgotten. It's better that way."

I squeezed my hands into tight fists as I forced myself to take a deep breath. If one more person told me that not knowing something was for my own good, I might start screaming and never stop. "Yes, I've heard that as well. Although it makes no sense to me. Why would everyone be so terrified of a group of criminals that vandalize, steal, and do drugs? It's not like they're murdering people."

"That we know of," Mildred said.

I widened my eyes. "What? Are you seriously telling me that in a town the size of Redemption, we might have some group running around murdering people, and no one is talking about it?"

Mildred looked at me in exasperation. "Charlie, you've lived here long enough to know that not everything is as it seems. And besides, you're forgetting about the powers."

I stared at her, not sure I had heard her correctly. "Powers? What are you talking about?"

"You know, powers." Mildred fluttered her fingers, as if she were casting a spell.

She couldn't be serious. "You mean like ... magic?"

Mildred's eyes widened before she quickly searched the dining area again, ensuring no one else had snuck up on us since the last time she checked. "Shhh, not so loud. You don't know who is listening."

"Didn't you just say that most of the rumors surrounding The Forgotten are nonsense?" I asked as she gave the young man in the beret a hard look. He didn't notice, as he was still madly scribbling in his notebook.

"Yes, I did, but the problem is figuring out what's nonsense and what's not." She gave one last disapproving look at the young man before finally turning back to me, leaning in close and lowering her voice. "I've heard stories you wouldn't believe. Like how they can control people."

I frowned. "Control people? You mean like blackmail them?"

She shook her head. "No, like *control* them. Using their minds." She pointed to her forehead.

I blinked. "Um … okay."

"Also, they can move objects around just by using their minds."

Oh for Pete's sake. "Can they fly, as well?"

She tapped her lower lip. "I haven't heard that one, but I wouldn't put it past them. Although, a few days ago, there was something flying around in my backyard. At first, I thought it was an owl, but it seemed a little too big for a bird."

I did my best to keep my expression neutral. "Owls are pretty big."

Mildred gave me a look like I had completely missed the point. "They're not six feet big."

I stared at her. "You're telling me you saw something that was six feet tall flying around in your backyard."

She flapped her hands. "I can't be sure how big it was. It wasn't like I had a ruler."

"But you just said it was six feet tall."

"And it might very well have been six feet tall!" She removed the spoon from her coffee, tapping it a couple of times at the edge and putting it on the wooden table. "Oh, they can also raise the dead."

My jaw dropped. "Raise the dead? You mean like zombies?"

"As far as I know, we haven't had any zombies in Redemption," Mildred said solemnly as she tasted her coffee. I had assumed she was kidding, but then I realized she was serious. "Although there was a feral cat in our neighborhood that I had my suspicions about."

I held out a hand. "Hold on. You're serious about this? Why would they have powers? Are they like … witches or something?"

"Men can't be witches," Mildred said. "The correct term would be warlocks."

I blinked. I had meant it as a joke, but Mildred looked as if she were taking me seriously. "You think they're warlocks?"

"As I said, they can't be witches," Mildred said, resting her elbows on the table as she held her coffee. "Although it's possible they would refer to themselves as sorcerers or magicians."

"I wasn't serious about them being witches … or warlocks or sorcerers or any of that," I said.

"Then why did you ask if they were witches or not?"

"Because you said they have powers," I said, trying not to let my exasperation show. "What else would they be?"

Mildred gave me a thoughtful look. "They could be oungans."

I stared at her. I had thought my question rhetorical and hadn't really expected a response. "What?"

"Oungans," she said conversationally, as if we were simply exchanging pleasantries about the weather. "That's what they call men who are voodoo priests."

"You think they're practicing voodoo?"

"Well, *somebody* created that zombie cat," Mildred said, sipping her coffee. "Although, I suppose it's also possible it wasn't The Forgotten who had the powers, but something they summoned."

"Summoned?" How did I get myself into this conversation? "What exactly would be summoned?"

Mildred waved one of her hands. "You know. The usual."

"Usual?"

"Spirits, demons, that sort of thing."

I rubbed my forehead, feeling the beginnings of a headache start to curl around my temple. "I can't believe this. Are you really telling me that everyone is afraid of The Forgotten because they think they have these powers?"

Mildred looked at me in surprise. "I thought you knew the history of The Forgotten."

I thought I did, too, but now, I was starting to wonder. "Why don't you tell me in case I don't know it all."

"I don't know if anyone who isn't an 1888er knows everything," Mildred said. "They don't like talking to us, but you already know that. My understanding is that The Forgotten are 1888ers who are trying to reverse the curse by tapping into whatever cursed them in the first place."

"And that gives them powers?"

"Temporarily. At least I think it's temporary." Mildred suddenly didn't look all that sure. "All I know is everyone is afraid of The Forgotten, and The Forgotten never last long."

I felt something cold at the back of my neck. There must be a draft somewhere. I shivered and folded my arms across my chest. "What happens to them?"

Mildred shrugged. "Impossible to know. They could die, they could be eaten by a zombie cat, or they could just walk away from being The Forgotten and just be regular 1888ers. It's not anything that's talked about outside of the 1888ers."

Suddenly, all the talk about The Forgotten's powers was making more sense. If there was one thing I had learned in my short time in Redemption, it was that the townspeople were highly superstitious. Even though I knew it was all nonsense (of course no one actually had any actual powers), if everyone *thought* they did, I could both understand the fear and also see why no one wanted to talk about them. "So how do The Forgotten get these supernatural powers?"

"I would imagine through occult practices," Mildred said.

Even though I had been expecting an answer like that, it still sent chills down my spine. "What occult practices?"

"You know. The usual."

I went back to rubbing my forehead to avoid tearing my hair out. "Indulge me. What are some examples of the usual?"

Mildred looked slightly offended. "How should I know? I don't have anything to do with occult practices."

I briefly closed my eyes. "Are there things you've heard that The Forgotten do?"

"Oh, heavens yes." Mildred took another sip of her coffee. "Rituals mostly. Many of them involving sacrifices."

This didn't sound good. "Sacrifices? Like … animal sacrifices?"

Mildred seemed to freeze for a moment. "And worse." She glanced around the coffee shop again. "Fire, too." Suddenly, her eyes brightened, and she sat up. "Wait. Is that what this is about? The fire?" She slapped herself on the side of her forehead. "I can't believe I didn't see the connection sooner. The Forgotten have always had a fascination with fire."

"What do you mean?"

"Many of their rituals involve fire. At least, that's what I've heard." She sipped her coffee, her expression pensive. "I always thought it was connected to Fire Cabin somehow, but maybe there's something else going on."

Fire Cabin was one of Redemption's many myths. According to the legend, located somewhere in the woods surrounding Redemption was what appeared to be a cabin perpetually on fire. If you found it, which was easier said than done as it also seemed to move locations, you'd either have your deepest wish granted … or your worst nightmare realized. While some had disappeared after supposedly finding Fire Cabin, others died. A year before, I'd met a group of five friends who had decided to take one final camping trip together to see if they could find Fire Cabin.

It didn't end well. Only four emerged from the woods.

"I never heard that The Forgotten were linked to Fire Cabin," I said. All I knew was that the cabin was somehow linked to what happened to the adults who disappeared in 1888.

Mildred rolled her eyes. "Are you kidding? Everything in Redemption is linked to the 1888ers, including The Forgotten." She tilted her head, her eyes narrowing. "And apparently, to 88 Spirits burning down."

I made a show of looking around the coffee shop and dropped my voice. "That's why it's so important not to tell anyone. We don't want to do anything to hurt an active investigation." I told myself it wasn't exactly a lie, as I didn't know what sort of investigation was open, only that Wyle wasn't a part of it.

Her head bobbed. "Of course. You can trust me."

The jury was still out on that. "That's why I need to know who is part of The Forgotten. Can you help?"

"Of course," Mildred said before immediately frowning. "Although I didn't even know there was a Forgotten group running around." Her frown deepened as she tapped her finger against the table. "I should have known something was up when that cat appeared."

I made a mental note to ask Wyle to see if he could get animal control out to Mildred's neighborhood to pick up any strange-looking feral cats. I had a feeling if I didn't, we might find Mildred out there one night trying to stab it with a stake or something. "But you knew at least some of the 1888ers when they were kids, right? Did any of them seem like they might become a Forgotten? Or are there any who might be willing to tell us who The Forgotten are?"

Mildred sat back in her chair as understanding flashed across her face. "Edie is involved, isn't she?"

"What?" That I didn't expect.

Mildred wasn't listening. Instead, she was shaking her head. "Oh, I should have known. Is that what this is about? Did she become a Forgotten?"

"I …" I hadn't thought about that, but reflecting on the conversation, it was certainly possible she had been a former member. Maybe that was why they were coming after her—they wanted her back in the fold. "Why would you say that?"

Mildred sighed and picked up her coffee. "Stupid child." But her voice wasn't so much judgmental as sad. "She had a tough life. By the time she was sixteen she'd lost both her parents. That would be tough for anyone, but for Edie …" Mildred shook her head.

"What do you mean?"

Mildred turned her head to gaze at one of the oak-hewn walls covered with artwork by local artists. The one she seemed to be looking at was a lovely watercolor painting of an English flower garden. "There was something delicate about her. Fragile, almost. Even before her parents' deaths. I was so worried about her … that she would just …break. But she didn't. At least not on the outside. After the initial shock, she came back to class and eventually graduated on time. I was really surprised, as I was sure she would completely fall apart. But …" Mildred turned back to me, her eyes intense. "Maybe she did break after all. And found something … dark to put herself back together."

Chapter 14

I shifted uneasily in my chair. "So you think she might have been the leader of The Forgotten?"

"It's possible," Mildred said, swallowing the last of her coffee and placing her cup on the table. "Grief does all sorts of things to people."

That was a little too close for comfort. "Do you remember who her friends were?"

Mildred furrowed her brow. "I don't remember anyone in particular. If I recall, she hung out with the other 1888ers, which tracks. But let me go through my files and see if anyone pops up."

"Do you remember Edie's last name and maybe when she graduated?" Listening to Mildred had given me an idea.

Mildred screwed up her face. "Fischer, I think. Or maybe it was Weber. No, I'm pretty sure it was Fischer."

Oh boy. Luckily, Redemption was pretty small, so I could look up both.

"What about when she graduated?"

"Had to be at least four or five years ago." That worked with how old she looked now. "When I find her records, I'll know for sure."

Finally. A helpful piece of information I could do something with.

***

I pushed open the doors of the Redemption Public Library, taking a moment to breathe in the familiar scents of paper and soft, leather, comfy cushions. Growing up, I used to love going to the library, even if the rest of my family never understood. My parents were always too busy to read, either working a million hours (my father) or climbing the New York social ladder (my mother). My sister, Annabelle, liked to read, but only new books that she bought at the bookstore. And my sister Marguerite's definition of reading was flipping through fashion or gossip magazines.

But to me, the library was always a sanctuary, maybe because the rest of my family had such an allergy to it. Being able to spend the day surrounded by books and not having to deal with the responsibilities of having been born a Kingsley was like a long, relaxing exhale.

The library was mostly empty, sans an older, balding man still wearing his winter jacket and a black wool cap sitting at one of the long wooden tables with a newspaper laid out in front of him. A librarian who didn't look much older than me, with her long, reddish-brown hair plaited in two messy braids, no makeup, and a tiny gold stud in her nose that matched her gold-rimmed glasses sat behind the counter. But she was dressed like the old man in jeans, a white turtleneck, and a thick, oversized, gray fisherman's sweater. It was so bulky, I wondered if she was also wearing additional layers under the turtleneck.

She smiled as I approached, peering at me over her glasses. "Can I help you?" I noticed she wore a small nametag with the name Vivian printed on it.

"Do you happen to have copies of the Redemption high school yearbooks?" Talking to Mildred had made me realize how little I knew about Edie, the only survivor, and while I hoped Mildred would find some names of Edie's friends or acquaintances, I felt like actually seeing photographs of Edie and her classmates might be even more insightful.

I wasn't sure if the public library would have copies of the high school yearbooks, but I thought it was worth a trip. My time in Redemption had shown me that small towns do things differently from big cities. Plus, I thought I would raise fewer eyebrows showing up at the public library versus the one at the high school. Not to mention, I doubted they would even let me into the school library.

If Vivian was surprised by my request, she didn't show it. "Yes, they're in the reference section. I can show you." She slid off her stool and gestured for me to follow her. "We're supposed to have a copy of all of them, but I think they only go back thirty years or so."

"Supposed to?"

"That's the agreement, but I'm not sure how well it's been followed. Also, depending on what year you're looking for, it's possible it might be missing. I know the last time I catalogued them, I noticed a couple years weren't there." She flashed me a quick smile. "I'm Vi, by the way. I know my nametag says Vivian, but no one calls me that."

I couldn't help but smile back. "Charlotte here, but everyone calls me Charlie." Everyone but my sister Annabelle, that is, but I didn't need to get into all of that unpleasantness. Annabelle had never understood how I could have possibly chosen a small midwestern town over New York City, and I think she was still waiting for me to come to my senses and move back.

"Charlie is much cuter than Charlotte," she said as she ran a finger over the shelves. "Ah, here they are." She stepped back with a flourish.

"Thanks." I wasn't sure if I would have thought to look for the yearbooks there, flanked by a complete Encyclopedia Brittanica set on one side and law reference texts on the other.

She took a step back. "Is there anything else I can help you with?"

"No, I think this is good for now. Thanks."

I was wondering if she was going to ask me what I wanted with high school yearbooks, and I already had my story ready—that I was doing some research as my niece and nephew might be attending. Never mind that they were both toddlers. If she asked about their ages, I could gloss over it.

But she didn't. She simply smiled again and disappeared to presumably resume her spot behind the counter.

It didn't take me long to locate four out of the five volumes I wanted. I thought I would start with four years ago and go back from there, but unfortunately, one year smack in the middle was missing. An uneasy feeling stirred in my gut, but there wasn't much I could do about it other than try to track it down at the high school library. I took the pile of books to a nearby table, where I could spread out. I removed my coat and settled in.

It didn't take long to find her. Her name was Edie Fischer, and she had graduated five years before, which made her twenty-three. I had yearbooks from her senior, junior, and freshman years. Her sophomore year was missing.

I pushed down the uncomfortable feeling as I flipped through to find her senior picture. Even though it was only five years ago, she looked a lot younger. Part of it may have been that her face wasn't puffy from either the pregnancy or fire or grief (or all three). But there was also an innocence about her that seemed to be missing now, with her sandy brown hair swept into a complicated updo and quite a bit of makeup. She was smiling slightly for the camera, a smile that didn't match her eyes. There was a sadness about her that broke my heart. So much grief in someone so young.

I began to flip through the photos of all the various organizations, with zero expectations of seeing Edie in the smiling group photos (or any of the 1888ers, even if I had known who they were). They didn't strike me as big "joiners." I was hoping to find her in one of the candid photo collages that were placed throughout the book.

Which was why I almost missed her.

It was a small group of maybe eight people in a classroom along with an older man I assumed was the teacher in charge. The headline read "Alternative Newspaper: Tales From The Other Side."

The photograph was black and white. There were three girls, including Edie, and five boys. The boys were on one side and the girls on the other, although I noticed that Edie was standing a little apart from everyone else. There was another forced smile on her face, but the camera was far enough away that I couldn't get a good look at her eyes. Perhaps she just hated having her picture taken.

But what really drew my eye were the boys—one in particular. He was leaning against the desk, arms crossed, a smirk on his face. Just by looking at his body language, it was clear that he was the leader. He was also movie star handsome with his dark eyes and shaggy haircut. I shivered a little as I studied him. A bad boy if I had ever seen one. Every mother's worst nightmare.

His name was Bo Wagner, and I immediately flipped through to find his senior photo. But it was missing. I flipped through the rest of the yearbook, but I wasn't able to find another photo of either Bo or Edie.

I then went through the other two yearbooks, but there were no other photos of either of them. Both yearbooks mentioned Tales From The Other Side, but only one had a photo, and it didn't show them, either.

I took a moment to shelve the other yearbooks but kept Edie's senior year out. I put on my jacket and slipped the book under it. I felt a little guilty sneaking it out of the library, but not guilty enough to create a paper trail. Even though it made no sense, I couldn't shake the feeling that it would be a bad idea to officially check it out. I told myself it was okay, as I fully planned to return it after I was done with the case.

As I walked out (a little stiffly, as the book was bulky), Vi smiled at me. "Did you find what you were looking for?"

"Not exactly," I said. "But I appreciate your help."

"Of course," she said. "Anytime. That's what the library is here for."

***

A small bell jangled merrily as I pulled open the door to The Redemption Detective Agency. Mildred had called shortly after I returned home from the library, asking if I could meet her there. "It's safe," she said. I assumed that meant we would be alone, but as I stepped inside, I was thinking that might have been a bad assumption.

The Redemption Detective Agency was located in a strip mall alongside a pawn shop and used bookstore—Nora's, in fact, who was a "detective" at the agency. The space used to house a succession of failed restaurants, which was both a good and a bad thing. Good, because the rent was dirt cheap, but bad, as the space was wholly unsuited for a detective agency. In what would have been the dining area, there were four workstations set up, along with a few additional chairs. A long, built-in counter at the back, which was probably the waitress's station before, now supported a coffee maker and a small fridge. There was also a swinging door that had likely led to the kitchen, though I was unsure what it was being used for now.

Mildred was sitting behind the desk in the back corner waving wildly at me. "Over here!" she called out, although I wasn't sure where else I would have gone, as she was the only one there.

Well, her and a big yellow lab, who got up from his dog pillow and moseyed over to greet me. "Hi Scout," I said as I petted him. There was also a calico cat sleeping in the cat tree.

"Where is everyone?" I asked after removing my coat and hanging it up on the coat rack.

Mildred waved her hand. "Oh, don't worry about them. Emily and Tilde are out for a bit, so I thought it was safe for you to come by."

That was reassuring. Maybe Mildred really would keep this to herself after all.

I sat down in the folding chair across from Mildred, who began moving piles of paper around. "From what I can tell, Edie was mostly a loner, but she did have a couple of friends … or at least girls she would hang out with from time to time. Diane Schultz and Hazel Drexler. They were both 1888ers."

I sat up a little straighter. Both of them had been pictured in the Tales From The Other Side group.

"Unfortunately, I wasn't able to locate either of them. Neither are listed in the phonebook, and when I called their parents' numbers, the phone just rang and rang."

"No answering machine?"

Mildred straightened her glasses. "No, which was why I thought we could go over to their houses and see what we could discover."

My eyes widened. "*We?*"

Mildred peered at me over her glasses. "Well, I assumed you would want to come, too."

Apparently, I was going to have company that afternoon. "What about any boys?"

Mildred gave me a funny look. "Boys?"

I produced the yearbook and started flipping through it.

Mildred gave me a look that was somewhere between shocked and rueful. "You got a yearbook? From where? I should have thought of that."

I ignored her question. "Have you heard of this group? Tales From The Other Side?" I found the page and turned it to show her.

She gave me a very stern look, and I could feel myself wilt inside. I felt like I was back in elementary school waiting for the teacher to punish me. I was practically bracing myself for her to yell at me, but instead, she simply pulled the yearbook toward her to get a closer look at the photo. "Ohhh, those boys." Her voice was thick with disapproval.

"Who are they?"

"Trouble." She shook her head disapprovingly before looking up at me. "I can't believe Edie got involved with them. I thought she was smarter than that."

"Were they 1888ers?" I asked.

"That whole group was. Mr. Hildebrandt," she nodded toward the photo, "was the one who spearheaded this 'alternative newspaper.'" She put air quotes around the words alternative newspaper, and her expression made me think it either wasn't all that alternative or that much of a newspaper. I suspected the latter. "He wasn't an 1888er, but was related to them somehow … I think by marriage. He thought it was important to give them a group of their own that they would feel comfortable joining."

"Was this all the 1888er students, or were there others who didn't join?"

"There were never that many 1888er students attending at any one time, but I'd have to compare my notes to know if that was all of them or not. It seems to me most, if not all of them, were a part of that group." She removed her glasses and rubbed her face. "Oh, Edie. What have you gotten yourself into?"

Without her glasses, she looked younger and borderline vulnerable. I decided I needed to stop assuming the worst about her. "Tell me about the boys."

She pressed her lips together. "Hoodlums. All of them. Especially him." She stabbed her finger on Bo's smug picture and muttered something uncharitable under her breath.

"I take it he was the leader."

"Absolutely. That boy had way too much charm and was way too good-looking by half. You just knew he was going to end up in trouble."

"Did he?"

She made a face. "Not to my knowledge. Some of the others, who weren't nearly as slick, weren't so lucky."

"What did they do?"

She shook her head. "What didn't they do? Vandalism, theft, drugs. One even brought a knife to school. He ended up getting expelled."

"One of these guys?" I pointed to the picture.

She adjusted her glasses and squinted at the photo. "I don't think it was any of them, but I'm going to have to check for sure."

"Do your files include all of these boys' addresses?" I asked.

She looked up at me, and a slow smile spread across her face. "Absolutely. Let me get my coat."

Chapter 15

"You're sure this is the right place?" I asked again.

Mildred squinted at the piece of paper she held in her gloved hand. "Positive. We're at 126 Birch Street, right?"

I frowned as I glanced toward the mailbox. "We're at 128 Birch Street."

Mildred held the paper closer to her nose. "Oh, right. 128."

I restrained myself from snatching the paper from her so I could check it myself and took a deep breath instead.

It had been an unproductive afternoon. Mildred and I visited about a half-dozen houses, but no one was home. At least, no one answered the door. I wouldn't put it past any of them to have been hiding behind a curtain and watching us as we rang their doorbell.

We had been slowly working our way down the list, having started with the two girls, and were now at Milo Kiefer's residence, one of the boys in the photo.

"I'm sure this is his house," Mildred said.

I stared at the large, two story, well-kept (despite its age) residence. It seemed a little much for a young man in his early twenties. "Is this Milo's house, or his parent's?"

"It's his. Or at least where he's living now," Mildred said.

I rang the doorbell again, although I didn't have much faith anyone would answer, and looked around the property. There was a detached two-car garage off the side of the house. I went to take a closer look, as Mildred hastily flipped through sheets of paper, muttering to herself. Maybe I could see if there were any cars in the garage or if there was an apartment I wasn't seeing.

As I got closer, I didn't see an apartment, but I did see a worn path that led to the side of the house and a set of stairs going below ground to what was presumably a basement.

"Well, I guess we can try Conrad next," Mildred said, but her voice didn't sound very hopeful.

"Actually, I think there might be a basement apartment," I called out.

Mildred looked up. "How do you know he's debasing anyone?"

"A basement apartment," I said again, slowly enunciating each word. I gestured for her to follow me as I headed toward the stairs.

It was immediately clear that the concrete stairs had been recently used, as they were clear of any snow and ice. There were multiple cracks and chips throughout, and they led to a small landing with a grate in front of a plain wooden door. I carefully grasped the black, wrought iron handrail as I made my way down, Mildred following close behind me.

"You really think he's living down here?" Mildred asked skeptically. "It doesn't seem very safe."

I suspected the word "safe" never entered the head of a twenty-something man. "We'll find out," I said as I pushed the button that I assumed was the doorbell. It rang out a deep, old-fashioned chime.

To my surprise, I heard scuffling sounds from inside before the door flew open.

"Can I help you?" A young man stood in the doorway, arms crossed over his chest, eyeing both of us suspiciously. His jaw dropped when he saw Mildred. "Uh ... is that you, Ms. Schmidt?"

Mildred straightened up. "It is indeed."

His eyes widened, and he looked as if he wasn't sure what to say. He wasn't half bad looking, with light-brown hair, pale-blue eyes, and obvious, well-developed chest muscles despite the baggy red sweatshirt. "Um ... what are you doing here?"

Her expression was stern. "What is this nonsense I'm hearing about you being a part of The Forgotten?"

Oh no. I briefly closed my eyes, wishing I could become Alice in Wonderland and shrink into a form tiny enough to fit into that grate. I had assumed we were going to start by asking about the fire. I thought I could say something, as I had been there, then segue into

Edie and maybe, if we were lucky, ask about The Forgotten. But, no, Mildred jumped right into the deep end.

I made a mental note to ensure I discussed strategies more thoroughly with her in the future.

Milo went very pale, and his mouth dropped open. "Um …" Behind him, I saw two other young, well-built men, and it suddenly occurred to me I was standing at the bottom of a concrete staircase with an elderly woman, and no one knew where we were.

I definitely hadn't thought this through.

Mildred, however, had none of those thoughts as she put both hands on her hips and glared at Milo. "I have to say I'm very disappointed in you."

"Who said anything about The Forgotten?" One of the young men poked his head out from behind Milo. His blonde hair was in desperate need of a cut, as it kept falling into his eyes.

"Conrad? Are you a part of this nonsense as well?" Mildred asked.

Conrad instantly looked contrite. "Ah, no … no ma'am."

"And who else is with you?" Mildred asked, craning her neck to look behind them. "You. You look familiar."

"Oh, I get that a lot," he said with a smirk. His face remained shadowed, so I couldn't get a good look. But from what I could tell, there was a hardness about him that was missing from the other two boys. Unconsciously, I took a step back and bumped into the concrete wall. His smirk deepened, and I could almost feel his eyes on me, even though I couldn't quite see them.

I didn't seem to the only one he made uncomfortable. Conrad glanced nervously at him before shifting a step away from him, as well. "Why are you asking about The Forgotten?"

I quickly jumped in before Mildred could. "So The Forgotten IS back."

His eyes widened in panic. "Wait. I didn't …"

"And who might you be?" Smirk asked, tilting his head.

Ugh. I really didn't want to tell any of these boys my name. On the other hand, they already knew who Mildred was, so it probably didn't matter. "Charlie. And you are …"

He folded his arms across his chest. "A concerned friend."

I narrowed my eyes. "So what do I call you? A, or maybe Concerned?"

His smirk turned into a grin. "You can call me whatever you want, darling."

"Enough of that," Mildred snapped, stepping forward. "Where's Bo?"

There was an uncomfortable silence. "Bo?" Milo asked. It seemed to me he looked paler than before, but it was difficult to tell, as there wasn't much light.

"Yes, Bo," Mildred said, craning her neck to see further into the apartment. "Is he back there somewhere too?"

Conrad swallowed hard. His left eye had started to twitch. "Bo is dead."

"What?" Mildred stared at him before pressing a hand to her mouth that had fallen open. "Bo is dead? Bo Wagner?"

"Yes ma'am," Conrad said. Smirk looked down as he shuffled his feet, his face lost to the darkness.

"I can't believe it." Mildred's expression had turned gray. "What happened?"

Conrad cleared his throat before glancing at Milo, who was staring at the ground. "Car accident. Um … they think he was drinking and driving."

"Oh Bo," Mildred said, shaking her head as Smirk nudged Conrad in the back. Conrad's mouth snapped shut. "How could you not learn that you shouldn't drink and drive? Was anyone else hurt?"

"No ma'am," Conrad started to say, but Smirk suddenly stepped forward, pushing him to one side and causing him to stumble into Milo.

"Why are you asking so many questions?" Smirk asked, his dark eyes glinting as he gave both of us a hard look. "What does Bo have to do with The Forgotten?"

There was something so aggressive in his demeanor that I tried to take another step back. No luck, though, as I was already against the concrete. I could feel the coldness from the stone seeping into my jeans. "Who said that Bo and The Forgotten were related?"

His eyes were like lasers, cutting into mine. Now that he had moved more into the light, I was able to get a better look at him. There was a sharpness about his features, all angles and high cheekbones and a hooked nose, almost reminding me of a hawk. His hair was a warm auburn, soft and wavy as it curled around his pointed chin, and the color of his eyes was like warm liquid gold. It was almost disconcerting to see the hardness of his face next to the softness of his hair and eyes. "What, you think I'm stupid? Why are you here asking about Bo and The Forgotten, if it isn't related?"

Oh boy. This was definitely not going well. Even Mildred had fallen quiet next to me. I could feel her thin body pressed against my side. "We're just helping out a friend."

Smirk's eyes narrowed. "A friend? Right." He took another step toward us, and I could see one of his hands clench into a fist. "You're working with Edie, aren't you?"

"What?" I couldn't hide my utter shock. "How … why …?"

He gave me a disgusted look. "Again, stop thinking we're stupid. There's only one thing that's happened in this godforsaken town recently, and that was 88 Spirits burning down."

I had to admit he had a point, even if I didn't like the way he was making it. Again, I thought about how no one knew where we were. Why didn't I call Wyle? I could have at least left him a message about what Mildred and I were doing. But kicking myself about it wasn't going to do anything to get Mildred and I out of the current situation. I was going to have to try to bluff my way out. I forced myself to straighten up and square my shoulders. "What have you heard about the fire?"

"Wait, you said your name was Charlie, right?" Milo said. "Were you the one at the fire?"

Ugh. I was hoping they didn't put two and two together. "Yes. That's why I'm here."

Smirk's face tightened. "You were the one at 88 Spirits?" He took another step toward us, both of his fists now clenched. "You've talked to her, haven't you?"

"Who?" I asked.

Conrad glanced at Smirk, his brow creased. "Hey man, maybe we should lay off?"

Smirk shrugged him off, his eyes never leaving mine. "You know who," he hissed.

Now both Conrad and Milo were giving Smirk uneasy looks, which actually wasn't making me feel any better. "Come on man, you're scaring them," Milo said.

"Arthur's wife is the one who asked me to look into the fire," I said. I felt a split second of guilt twist through me as the words left my mouth. It certainly wasn't my intention to put Carol on this man's radar, but I had a feeling if he was planning on bothering Carol, he would already have done so. Whatever I said or didn't say wasn't going to make any difference. Edie, though, was a whole different story. "As you can imagine, she'd like to get to the bottom of what happened to her husband and his bar."

He stayed where he was, still staring at me. The tension was so thick, it felt like I was being buried alive. "If you didn't talk to Edie, how did you find us?"

I raised an eyebrow. "You think Edie is the only person who would connect you to The Forgotten?"

Silence. I pressed my hands against the sides of my body, trying to keep them from visibly trembling. From behind Smirk, I could see Milo and Conrad shoot each other uneasy looks.

Finally, Smirk took a step back. "I don't know where you got your information, but we don't know anything about The Forgotten. Right, boys?" He didn't look at either Milo or Conrad, as he was still watching me, but that didn't stop them from quickly agreeing.

I forced a smile onto my face. "Alright then. I don't suppose you know who might be involved with The Forgotten?"

"I have no idea," Smirk said. Instantly, I knew he was lying.

Mildred apparently did too. "Then who let that zombie cat loose in my neighborhood?"

Smirk blinked and looked completely caught off guard. "What?"

"Somebody turned your cat into a zombie?" Conrad asked.

"Why would you want to turn my cat into a zombie? I don't even have a cat," Mildred said in her most frightening teacher's voice.

"No, we would never do that," Milo said hastily.

"Honestly, we would never turn your cat into a … a zombie," Conrad said.

Mildred took a step forward as she shook a finger. "Then who is turning the neighborhood cats into zombies? I want a name, right now!"

"Nobody turned anyone's cat into a zombie," Smirk said, but he didn't seem as sure of himself as he had before. He gave both Milo and Conrad a funny look. "The Forgotten being able to raise the dead is a myth."

"If not The Forgotten, then who?" Mildred demanded.

"Check with Doc," Smirk said as he stepped back inside. "We have to go." The other two quickly followed him right before the door slammed shut.

Chapter 16

It took a moment before I felt steady enough to push away from the cold concrete wall, even though every part of me was screaming to get out of there as fast as possible. But when the door slammed shut, it felt like all of the bravado drained out of my system, leaving my knees weak and wobbly.

"Those boys are absolutely up to no good," Mildred fumed before turning toward the stairs. "Coming?"

"Yes," I said, forcing myself off the wall and hurrying after her. "Who is Doc?"

"I assume the doctor in town, but I don't think he knows anything about voodoo," Mildred said. "At least I've never heard of him creating zombies." While the words were something Mildred would say, her voice sounded far away, like she was thinking of something else.

"Did you recognize that third guy?" I asked.

She didn't immediately answer. "Did you bring the yearbook with you?"

"Yeah, it's in my car." We had almost reached our vehicles parked on the street next to the curb. Mildred had wanted to drive separately "just in case," although I wasn't sure what the "just in case" was. I gestured toward my car, but Mildred stayed where she was. The dying sun was starting to cast long shadows against the dirty snow, and the wind was picking up. I tightened my coat around me.

"Is that the only yearbook? Or were there other ones as well?"

"There were others, although one was missing."

Mildred stilled. "Which one?"

"Um ..." I counted backwards. "I'm pretty sure it would have been Edie's sophomore year."

Mildred's expression shifted into one I couldn't read. "Oh, that's unfortunate. If I recall, the yearbook committee did a nice spread all about Edie that year."

I frowned. "They did?" I hadn't been expecting that. "Why?"

Mildred shook her head sadly. "It was such a shame. Edie lost both of her parents quite suddenly, and I think the school administration felt bad for her, as she was an only child. So they hosted a memorial service for Edie, and the yearbook committee ended up including a little tribute in the back of the book. I don't know how appropriate it was, as it was Edie's parents, not Edie, but their hearts were in the right place. I think people just didn't know what to do in that situation."

My head was spinning. Edie lost *both* of her parents in one year? "But I thought her parents died a few years apart? Her mom died of cancer, and her father had a heart attack …"

Mildred was staring at me as if I had grown a second head. "Who told you such nonsense? No, Edie's parents were in a car accident."

My eyes widened. "A car accident?" In my head, I could see Hattie again telling me about Edie's parents. There was definitely no mention of a car accident.

Mildred nodded. "It was a dreadful storm, and they think her father just lost control. There was some talk that he had been drinking, and there was other talk about someone having cut their brakes. But why would anyone kill them? Edie's parents were lovely people. And there was talk of the curse, of course." Mildred rolled her eyes. "I always felt bad for poor Edie. She not only had to deal with her parents' deaths, but all the gossip and innuendo, too. Eventually, it finally died down."

I murmured something about how unfortunate it was, but all I could think about was how Hattie had lied to me.

Of all things, why would she lie about that?

***

It was the next day when I found myself back on Hattie's porch.

I wasn't sure it was the right thing to do. I had argued with myself, as I was still worried that someone was going to see me visiting Hattie yet a third time and decide it was time to pay her a visit, as well. But I was also running out of options.

After Milo's house, Mildred and I split up. Mildred had gone home to see if she could figure out who the third person was, and I went home to give Wyle an update and try to get in touch with Hattie.

As it turned out, Hattie didn't answer her phone, and Wyle was less than impressed with the update.

"I don't think it's enough," Wyle finally said after I told him the whole story. I did, however, leave out the part about how menacing Smirk was. Well, and also the whole part about the zombie cat. Somehow, I didn't think Wyle would be amused.

My heart sank. "But I'm sure they're hiding something."

"I'm sure they probably are, but being sure isn't enough for a warrant. I need something a little more straightforward."

"What, like them confessing that they're Forgottens?"

I was mostly joking, but Wyle sounded serious. "That, or someone else identifying them as such."

I had no idea if I could get Edie to go on record identifying one of those guys as being a Forgotten, but I figured I had to try.

But what really bothered me was Hattie's lie. Why would she lie about how Edie's parents died? Was it possible that Hattie didn't remember what happened? No, I didn't believe that. While it was true that Hattie was getting up there in years, there was nothing wrong with her mind. I had never seen anything from her that indicated her mind not being sharp.

Was it because there appeared to be some questions surrounding the car crash? She wouldn't have to get into all of that with me, though. She could have just said Edie's parents died in a car crash, and that would have been the end of it.

The fact she didn't continued to gnaw at me.

And that gnawing, even more than Wyle wanting more evidence, was why I was on Hattie's front stoop again. Even while part of me fretted about putting them in danger.

I could see the blood drain from Hattie's face when she realized it was me. "Charlie. You shouldn't be here."

"Well, you shouldn't have lied to me," I said, pushing my way past her. It was easy to do, as she was so frail. The most difficult part was making sure I didn't knock her over. I slammed the door behind me and glared at her.

She took a step back, her hand grasping the collar of her dark-blue sweatshirt with a pink and green butterfly on it. Her hair looked better than when I was there a few days ago; it appeared as if she had washed and combed it, but she still looked a little too pale for my liking. "What are you talking about? We didn't lie to you."

"You lied about how Edie's parents died."

Her eyes widened, and she tightened her hand on her collar. "What? Didn't I tell you it was a car crash?"

I took a step toward her. "Don't play games with me. You know what you told me."

She swallowed hard. "I … I must have misspoke. Silly me." She forced a laugh. "But really Charlie, there was no reason to show up here for an honest mistake."

An honest mistake. I almost laughed, except this wasn't at all funny, especially after meeting Smirk in person. As much as I wanted to press her on why she lied, I knew I couldn't focus on that right now. Getting Wyle the information he needed to investigate was far more important. "Did Edie tell you who The Forgotten were?"

Hattie took another step back, her other hand reaching for the wall. Her face was so white, I was a little afraid she might collapse, and I subtly moved to catch her if she did. "We told you to leave that alone." She whisper-hissed the words.

"Just because you tell me to leave something alone doesn't mean the situation is contained," I said in my normal voice. "Where is Edie?"

"She's resting. You need to leave her be."

I doubted that, as the couch was empty, although I guess it was possible she was lying on Hattie's bed. I turned away from Hattie and headed to the kitchen. "Edie," I called out and promptly nearly ran into her.

"What do you want?" Edie was standing in the doorway. Her dark-green sweatshirt was stained, but it at least covered her belly. Her blue and white vertically striped pajama bottoms fit her better, as well. Her hair looked clean and was pulled back in a ponytail, but her eyes were hard.

"I need to know who The Forgotten are," I said.

Her face closed down. "As Hattie said, we told you to leave it alone. Besides, it's none of your business."

I took a step closer to her, close enough to smell the cheap shampoo and soap she had showered with. "It is my business if The Forgotten show up to finish the job they started at 88 Spirits."

Behind me, Hattie gasped, and Edie's face went pale, but she raised her chin and held my gaze. "Then maybe you shouldn't keep coming here, so the neighbors get suspicious."

Ugh. That hit home. But I couldn't let myself lose focus. "You really think they're just going to stop looking for you, even if I do?"

She winced. "What do you want?"

"I want to know who they are."

Her eyes shifted, so she was looking over my shoulder. "I can't tell you that."

"Why not?"

"Because they'll kill me."

Her words sounded almost as if they had been ripped out of her, raw and vulnerable. She pressed both of her hands against her belly.

"Charlie, do you see now?" Hattie asked, but I ignored her, taking a step closer to Edie and quieting my voice. "Then tell me who they are. Let me help you."

"You can't." Her voice was miserable. "Don't you understand? No one can. I just have to …" she paused, sucking in her breath and clenching her jaw.

"You have to what?" I prompted, but she shook her head. Some of her hair had dislodged from her ponytail, and it swept across her face like a curtain.

I was starting to get impatient again, even though I kept telling myself to be gentle. Clearly, she was already scared, and I didn't need to frighten her more. "So what are you going to do? Stay here indefinitely?"

"Edie can stay as long as she likes," Hattie said firmly, although Edie still refused to look at me.

"I'm sure she can, but that's not the point," I said. "If they're as dangerous as you say they are, don't you think they'll eventually find you here?"

"Charlie, don't say such things," Hattie snapped as Edie shuddered and closed her eyes, still gripping her belly. "Don't you think she's scared enough?"

This was going nowhere. "Was it Milo? Or Conrad?"

Edie's eyes flew open, and she staggered back a step. "What? How do you know Milo and Conrad?"

"Was it either one of them?"

"I …" She stared at me with a haunted expression, continuously rubbing her belly.

"There was a third guy with them. Auburn hair, golden eyes."

Edie's face jerked up toward mine, and she pressed both hands protectively around her belly. "What did you say?"

"Do you know who he is?"

She stumbled back another step. "I …"

I took another step toward her. "Is he part of The Forgotten?"

She kept limping backward, her face so ashen, I thought she might faint. "How do you know about him?" Her voice was barely a whisper, and there was something about her expression, or maybe in the way she kept cradling her baby, that caused something to finally click inside of me.

"Who is the father of your baby?"

She took another step backward, practically falling into one of the kitchen chairs. "What?"

"You heard me. Who is the father of your baby? Was it him?"

"Charlie, that's enough," Hattie said, jerking my arm. Edie was as far as she could get away from me, her eyes wild and face so pale, I was a little worried she had stopped breathing.

"Edie …" Oh man, had I pushed her too far? I tried to go to her, to help her, but Hattie jerked my arm a second time, with a surprising amount of strength. I nearly fell over, and by the time I righted myself, Edie had gotten herself to her feet and was lumbering her way out of the kitchen and toward the back of the house.

"I don't understand," I said to Hattie, who was trying to pull me toward the door. "Why won't you tell me what's going on? I'm trying to help you."

Hattie's mouth was a thin line. "You *can't* help us. The best thing you can do is leave us alone!"

"But this is no way to live," I said. "You've got to know the dangers, as well. If they come for her, you won't be able to protect her either."

"You don't think I know that?" Hattie's voice broke, and I saw she was close to tears. "But what else are we going to do?"

"What if I take her somewhere?" I asked. "My car is right outside."

"And go where?"

I lifted my hands. "A hotel. My house. What does it matter, so long as we can get her away from here?" What I didn't say was maybe we needed to take her to the police, but I had a feeling that would be too much of a stretch. If I could at least get her out of Hattie's house, it would be a first step to keeping both of them safe.

"I don't think she'll go," Hattie said.

"But why not? Doesn't she trust me?"

Hattie barked out a laugh that had no humor in it. "No, but that's not the reason. She thinks she'll be safer here."

I stared at Hattie, aware of her frailty, so riddled by arthritis she couldn't even clean her own home. For the life of me, I couldn't imagine what was going through Edie's head.

But then I reminded myself that this was a scared, pregnant, twenty-three-year-old who just lost a man who had tried to protect her. She obviously wasn't thinking straight … and could I blame her?

"I promise I'll take good care of her. And you, if she wants you to come, too. But if she's truly worried about her life, we need to get her moved to a more neutral location—one that will be more difficult for anyone to locate her. And we need to do it as soon as possible."

Something that resembled relief flickered in Hattie's eyes. Maybe someone just needed to take charge of this train wreck of a situation. "I'll talk to her. I don't know if she'll agree, but I'll see what I can do."

It was something. I would have preferred to be able to leave with Edie right then and there, but I would take what I could get.

Chapter 17

I was sitting at my kitchen table, a third cup of coffee in front of me along with half of a second muffin, trying to simultaneously wake up and shake my foul mood when the phone rang.

It had been a difficult night. Not only did I dream again of being cursed, trapped in a building being consumed by fire, but I'd also had a frustrating encounter with Wyle.

After leaving Hattie's, I went in search of Wyle to try to talk him into getting involved again. More and more, I was starting to feel like I was in way over my head. Edie and Hattie needed more protection than one tea maker could provide.

Wyle was just leaving the station when I pulled into the parking lot. My heart twisted as I watched him walk toward his car, his face drawn and haggard and badly in need of a shave. I kept the car running and the heat on as I beeped my horn and opened the car door to wave at him. His eyes lit up for a moment, but darkened almost as quickly, and he glanced furtively around the parking lot before joining me in the front seat of my car.

"You shouldn't have come," he said.

"I wanted to give you an update, but we can meet somewhere else if you'd be more comfortable," I said. "Maybe get some dinner." If anyone looked like they needed a hot meal, it was Wyle. I wondered when he had last eaten something other than fast food or microwaved meals. It was probably when he'd come over for breakfast a few days ago.

He hesitated, and I could almost see him considering it before his body deflated. "No, it's probably better this way. I have to be up early tomorrow for another double shift."

There was a stillness about him as he stared out the window into the darkening evening, his eyes hooded and watchful. Again, I could feel my heart twist inside me, but I couldn't pinpoint why. "How's work?"

"Fine." His answer was curt, and I immediately knew he was lying. I also knew he would never admit it. "So, what do you have for me?"

I quickly filled him in on what Edie had said about fearing for her life. I could see his expression grow grim as I talked. "So what do you think? Is that enough to open an investigation?"

It took him a few moments before he answered. "I'll see what I can do," he said at last. "Although it would be better if she came in and filed a formal complaint."

"That's not happening," I said.

He ran a hand through his hair. "Yeah, I figured as much." He let out a long sigh and eyed me. "I think you need to back off from this investigation."

It shouldn't have been a surprise, as I knew he didn't like me involved in cases under the best of circumstances, never mind when his hands were tied behind his back. But I still hadn't expected it. "What if it's not enough and you need more proof?"

"We'll cross that bridge when we get to it," he said. "But for now, I think it's time for you to back off. Stay away from Edie and Hattie."

Oh geez. I hadn't told him that I had offered to take Edie somewhere. This was going to be awkward, especially if Hattie happened to call to tell me that Edie was ready for me to pick her up. "Someone has to help them."

"And I said I would try," he said. "But Charlie, it's not your job to save people who don't want to be saved."

I felt as if I had been punched in the gut. "What are you talking about? Why would you think Edie doesn't want to be saved?"

His eyes were intense as he looked at me. "Is she asking the police for help?"

"She thinks the cops are corrupt. And quite honestly, after seeing how they've treated you, I'm not sure she's wrong."

He pressed his lips together tightly. "Has she done *anything* to help herself?"

"Well, she's hiding," I said, but even as the words left my mouth, I wondered if that was true. Yes, she was staying with Hattie, but was that really hiding? The other 1888ers must have known that Edie stayed with Hattie after her parents died.

"So you constantly showing up where she's hiding is what? Helpful?" His voice was sarcastic, and I bristled.

"That's not fair," I said. "You were the one who said you needed proof. What else was I supposed to do?"

Wyle dropped his gaze and started to rub his forehead. "I know. You're right. This is partially my fault too."

I blinked. I hadn't expected that, either.

"But Charlie," he said, lifting his gaze and staring at me again with that intensity that took my breath away. "That's why you have to back off. I don't have a good feeling about this at all."

Him and me both. But I also didn't think it was the time to admit that, especially since I wasn't sure I would be able to walk away. Hattie and Edie needed me—well, they needed someone, even if they didn't think they did. And no one else was stepping up to help them. So what choice did I have?

I couldn't say that to Wyle, though. Especially with the way he was looking at me, making my heart slam erratically inside my chest. He lifted a hand and brushed a strand of hair off my face, his touch so light against my cheek that I shivered, despite the heat being on high. "I couldn't deal with something happening to you."

My heart went from pounding so hard I could feel it in my temples to stopping. I couldn't breathe; I couldn't think. All I could do was stare into his dark eyes that had somehow turned even darker. I knew he felt the energy, too, and I could see his hesitation, as if he were mentally debating whether this was the time to step over the line that separated us from friendship and something more.

Every nerve ending inside me screamed to stop this. I couldn't get involved with Wyle. I couldn't get involved with any man. My past was too complicated, and if I let him step over this line, if I stepped over it with him, I risked losing our friendship. And that was too precious to me.

Even though it physically hurt, like I was tearing out a part of myself, I forced myself to turn my head away. I heard him sigh, so soft it was barely there, and then the shifting of the seat as he moved away from me.

"Does this mean you'll let this case go?" His voice was hoarse, and he cleared his throat a couple of times.

"Just as long as you'll be able to investigate those guys," I said. My voice sounded like his, and part of me wanted to kick myself. Was this what I really wanted? To push him away like that? Not particularly. But what choice did I have?

"I know Edie hasn't asked for help," I continued. "And I agree, she should be the one asking for it. But she's twenty-three, pregnant, and just barely survived a horrible experience. She's not thinking straight. I know she's not, and I can't just walk away without knowing someone is at least doing something."

There was a pause as Wyle considered my words. After a moment, he gave me a sideways smile. "Deal." But his eyes still looked concerned.

Now, sitting with my coffee after a night of tossing and turning (and dreaming of fire and curses), I kept thinking about his expression. How he had said he would "try" and investigate.

What if he couldn't?

What if he was shut down?

Then what? Was it up to me? And what should I do if Hattie did call—what if she told me Edie wasn't interested? Should I keep pushing it?

And when I wasn't trying to figure out how to handle Edie, I kept picturing that moment in the car, when Wyle pushed the hair out of my face. The look in his eyes. And I couldn't help but wonder if I had made a terrible mistake.

The ringing of the phone was a welcome distraction from my spiraling thoughts. I took my coffee with me to answer it, so I could top it off.

"Charlie, thank goodness you picked up." Mildred's voice came through the line. "I know his name."

I tucked the receiver between my shoulder and ear and reached for the coffeepot. "Whose name?"

"The one who was with Milo and Conrad."

My hand jerked, and I spilled coffee over the counter. I quickly replaced the pot before I could do any more damage. "Who is it?"

"His name is Troy Oslo." She sniffed loudly. "I should have figured it out sooner. He was always a troublemaker."

"What kind of trouble?" The name didn't ring a bell. Mentally, I went through all the people in the photo from the yearbook, but I didn't remember a Troy.

She snorted. "Everything. Drugs, fighting, stealing, vandalism. It would be faster to tell you what he *didn't* do."

"He's an 1888er, right? Why wasn't he in the yearbook photo?"

"Probably because he had been expelled by then."

All the hair on my body was standing up, and I had an awful feeling I wasn't going to like the rest of the conversation. "What did he do?"

"That's the thing." Her voice dropped, as if she didn't want to be overheard. I wondered where she was calling from. "I can't find that information."

"Why not?"

I could hear the frustration in her voice. "It's been removed from his records."

I reached for a washcloth to wipe the spilled coffee off the counter. "Is that normal?"

"No. Not at all." I heard the sound of paper rustling. "I don't know what to make of it."

"Do you know what happened to him after he was expelled?"

"Not yet. Normally, when students are expelled, they end up enrolling at an alternative high school, but I can't find any record of him at any of those." Her voice darkened. "I'm guessing he ended up in juvenile hall. Or maybe even jail."

All the coffee I had been drinking started sloshing around inside me, and I was starting to wish I hadn't drunk so much. "You think he might have just gotten out of prison?"

"Well, he certainly had that institutionalized look, don't you think?"

I thought back to his face, with his hard features and strange golden eyes. Was that the result of being behind bars?

I needed to call Hattie. I had to warn her and Edie. If all this was happening because Troy had just got out of prison …

I couldn't even finish that thought.

I asked Mildred to keep me posted on anything she found and hung up the phone. Scrambling to find Hattie's number, I jumped when the phone rang again. For a moment, I considered letting the answering machine take it while I kept looking for Hattie's number, but at the last second, I snatched it up. Maybe it was Wyle with some news. Or maybe it was Hattie, and she was going to tell me that Edie had agreed to let me take her somewhere safe.

"Hello?"

All I could hear was what sounded like sobbing.

I tried to keep the panic out of my voice. "Hello? Who is this?"

"Ch … Ch … Charlie?" I could barely understand the voice, it was so choked by tears.

"Yes, it's Charlie. Who is this?" My heart felt like it was being squeezed by an iron fist. "Hattie, is it you?"

"Charlie, they took her!"

The voice collapsed in fresh sobs. I could feel my knees start to wobble, and I sank to the floor. "Who? Who did they take?" Although I already knew the answer.

"Edie."

I closed my eyes and forced myself to breathe. I was too late. Even worse, it could all be my fault. What if I had led Troy and the other two to Edie? If anything happened to her or her baby, I might never forgive myself. "What happened?"

I could hear Hattie trying to get herself under control. "I'm not really sure. It was in the middle of the night, and I was fast asleep. I heard a scuffle from the living room, and Edie called out. I went out, and they had her."

"Who?"

"I … I'm not sure. They wore ski masks. But Edie knew who they were. I could tell."

"How many were there?"

Hattie's voice had steadied, as if talking about it was grounding her. "Two, I think. Maybe three? No, I think there were only two."

Only two. I wondered where the third one was. In my mind, I could see Conrad and Milo, neither of them looking happy with Troy. Did one of them refuse? Or had Troy found someone else to help?

"Then what happened?"

I could hear the threat of tears again in her shaky voice. "I tried to stop them, Charlie. Really, I did."

My heart broke. "I know you did. It's not your fault. None of this is your fault. Just tell me what happened."

"One of them hit me." Her voice hardened, and for a moment, I could hear the real Hattie—the Hattie who had become my tea customer, even though the community she had lived in her entire life frowned upon it. The Hattie who refused to bend to a curse that had broken that community. "Punched me in the face. I fell and hit the back of my head on something. I remember Edie screaming for them to leave me alone … and then I don't remember anything at all until I woke up a few minutes ago."

"Are you okay?"

"I'll live. My head is killing me, but don't worry about me. We have to find Edie."

I was worried about Hattie. I wasn't sure how long she had been unconscious, but it sounded like it had been several hours. She probably had a concussion, which meant she really needed to see a doctor. But I also knew that I would not win that argument. "Make yourself a pot of my tea—that should help with the pain and swelling. Double how much you normally drink. I'll bring more if you need it."

"I'm fine. It's Edie we have to worry about."

"Did you call the cops?" I wondered why I even bothered asking the question when I already knew the answer.

"No! I told you, no cops."

"But this is kidnapping. We need to get them involved."

"Absolutely not." Hattie's voice was firm. "We can't trust them. It's up to us to find her."

I squeezed the receiver tightly. I thought about the promise I had made to Wyle … the promise I was about to break. "I'll look for her. You stay put."

"I can help!"

"You can help by making yourself a pot of tea and resting," I said. "You need to get your strength back."

"I should have insisted she leave with you yesterday," Hattie fretted. "I had a bad feeling, but I didn't think it would happen so fast. I thought for sure we would have another day or two."

My throat tightened. "It's not your fault," I said. "If anything, it's mine."

I braced myself, waiting for her to scream at me, to tell me I should have listened to them and not poked into things that didn't concern me. If I hadn't gone to Milo's apartment … if I hadn't gone back to Hattie's house …

"It's not your fault." Hattie's voice was stronger. "You were right. It was silly for us to think we could simply hide in my house and not have this happen. They were bound to figure it out."

I swallowed hard as a complicated wave of guilt, fear, and relief washed over me. "Who is 'they'? I know you said you didn't recognize who took Edie, but do you have any idea who they might be?"

"Edie wouldn't tell me details, so I don't know for sure." Her voice was hesitant.

"Was it Milo and Conrad?"

More hesitation. "I just … I knew both of those boys their entire lives. I can't imagine they would be involved in something like that."

"What about Troy Oslo?"

There was a gasp. "So it was Troy with them!" Fear seeped into her voice. "Charlie, you need to stay away from Troy. He's dangerous."

"But if he has Edie, what am I supposed to do?"

"Oh, this is such a disaster," Hattie muttered.

"Maybe we should call the cops …"

"No! Absolutely not. Especially if Troy is involved."

"What are you talking about?

"There's no time." Hattie's voice was urgent. "Charlie, you have to find Edie. Once you find her, if you can get her away from Troy, then do it. But if you can't, then call me."

"Call *you*?" Oh geez, this was getting better and better. "What are *you* going to do?"

"Don't worry about that." Hattie's voice was like steel. "Just go find her. Before it's too late."

Chapter 18

As it turned out, telling me to find Edie was a lot easier than me actually finding Edie.

After I hung up with Hattie, I grabbed the yearbook, the phone book, a city map, and my few scribbled notes and headed out to the car. I considered calling Mildred back to see if she had any more information about Troy, but almost immediately decided against it. The last thing I wanted was Mildred insisting on coming with me. If Troy were as dangerous as I thought he was, Mildred was better off staying far away.

I did try calling Wyle, despite Hattie's insistence on keeping the police out of it. He wasn't at the station, though. A bored officer asked if I wanted to leave a message. After a brief hesitation, I said no and hung up. What message would I possibly leave? *Edie has been kidnapped, and I'm about to go look for her. Oh, and along with checking out Milo and Conrad, can you also see what you can find on Troy Oslo? Mildred thinks he's an ex-con, and Hattie is terrified of him, so naturally, I'm off to see if he took Edie.*

Yeah, that wasn't going to work.

Regardless, I couldn't shake the feeling that I was making a massive mistake not telling Wyle. Or the uneasy guilt that wouldn't go away no matter how many times I told myself I had tried to get a hold of him. What else was I supposed to do? It wasn't as if I had all sorts of time to waste trying to track him down. I had to find Edie.

Still, it didn't sit well with me.

I started by going back to Milo's basement apartment, hoping against hope they had brought Edie there. But of course, no one was home. I then circled around to all the other places I had visited with Mildred the day before, but again, no one was home. Or, at least, no one answered the door.

I could only find one Oslo who owned a house in the 1888ers' section of town. It was actually a pretty nice house—nicer than most in the area—pale-blue, two-story with black and white trim and what looked to be a decent-sized yard. But there was also a For Sale sign in the yard. I parked on the side of the road anyway, even though I doubted Troy would have brought Edie there. Still, it was possible someone living nearby knew where Troy was. However, I had just turned the car off when a vehicle pulled up behind me. It was a realtor. Her name was Cami, and everything about her was over the top—from her over-teased blonde hair to her makeup to the perfume she had doused on.

She thought I was the potential buyer she was supposed to be meeting for a walkthrough. After she found out I wasn't, she handed me her card and told me to call her office to make an appointment if I was still interested in viewing the house, assuming the potential buyer she was meeting didn't make an offer first.

"It's really a great deal. The owners are very interested in selling, so I wouldn't wait if you're in the market," she practically sang.

I thanked her and slipped her card into my purse. Even though a part of me was curious about the house and wouldn't mind going inside, I was a little afraid it would be a big waste of time … and time was something I didn't have. Even if this was Troy's childhood home, it seemed pretty obvious he hadn't been living there recently. And even if he had been, being able to do any serious poking around while a realtor was giving me a tour was unlikely.

Then again, if I wasn't able to locate Edie any other way, this might be my only lead.

I was now driving aimlessly around, not even sure what I was looking for. All I knew was that I had a growing sense of dread: if I didn't find Edie soon, I was going to be too late.

But I had no idea how to do that.

I turned right onto yet another neighborhood street. Like every other one I had driven down, it had an empty, deserted feeling to it. The houses were dark, with curtains tightly closed. If there was a car in the driveway or yard, it was broken down. No sign of a person anywhere. Not even a dog. Even the snow in the yards seemed untouched by humans. The only sign that anyone actually lived in any of them was that most of the driveways and sidewalks were shoveled.

It was starting to give me the creeps.

And it was also a waste of time. Did I really think I would stumble upon Edie this way? Like she would be standing in a front window, just waiting for someone to find her?

I needed a better plan. Maybe I needed to talk to Hattie again.

I reached for the map as I pulled over to the curb (not that it seemed to matter, as I had seen very few cars driving around). I wasn't entirely sure where I was. As I traced my location, I realized I was only a few blocks away from 88 Spirits.

Something shuttered inside me, almost as if I had poked a sleeping beast, and it was starting to awaken.

88 Spirits.

Where it all began.

But it was a burned-out husk. Why would Troy take Edie there?

Except ... what did Mildred say about fire and The Forgotten?

The Forgotten have always had a fascination with fire.

My skin felt like it was about to crawl off my body.

Edie's words came back to me. She had been in the basement before the fire started.

A basement.

Even if the rest of the bar was destroyed, it was possible the basement was still intact.

With shaking hands, I put the car back into drive and pulled out. I was being ridiculous. Chances were high that the floor had caved in, and there wouldn't be anything to find there, either.

Most likely, this was going to be like everything else I had tried—a giant dead end.

On the other hand, I didn't have any other ideas, so what did I have to lose?

***

I turned down the side street that led to 88 Spirits, or at least what was left of it, and immediately pulled over to the curb to park.

If Troy and whoever else was there, I didn't want my car giving them a heads-up to my arrival. It was only a couple of blocks away, and I decided I might have better luck sneaking up on them on foot.

I found myself jogging rather than walking. It felt like there was a giant clock in my head, ticking down the seconds, and I was terrified that, at any moment, it would hit zero, and Edie's luck would run out. I knew it made no sense. It wasn't as if I could actually know what was happening to her, but that made no difference to the mental clock.

Sweat started to trickle down my neck, even as the cold air slapped my face and burned my lungs. I pulled the glove off my right hand so I could unzip my jacket. The only sound I could hear was the thudding of my boots against the sidewalk. Like the rest of this particular part of town, there appeared to be no one around. Even the warehouse across the street looked deserted.

No wonder 88 Spirits was bleeding cash. I was starting to wonder if anyone, other than a handful of people like Hattie, actually lived here. Maybe it was some sort of weird Redemption joke.

I slowed down as the burned remains of 88 Spirits came into view, and my heart started to sink. There wasn't much left. Two walls, both charred black, were still standing, along with a few studs with yellow crime scene tape wrapped around them, ends fluttering in the breeze. The air was still filled with the stench of smoke and ash.

The closer I got, the more my heart clenched. I couldn't believe Edie was there. I couldn't believe anyone was there. Even though I could catch glimpses of floor that wasn't covered with burned-out wreckage, and that likely meant the basement was still more or less intact, I couldn't believe anyone would be there.

Another dead end.

And I was running out of time.

Nevertheless, since I was there, I was committed to checking it out. It wasn't like I had anything better to do. Other than heading back to the realtor, which felt like a long shot, all I could think to do was to start from the beginning and talk to Hattie and Carol again.

I circled around to the back of the building, careful not to slip on the blackened ice that had pooled around it. No snow, which made sense, as it had probably all melted with the heat of the fire and the water from the fire hoses.

It was so quiet, all I could hear was the crunch of my boots on the frozen ground and my own heavy breathing. I felt a little foolish poking around.

Near the cracked window where I had first seen Edie, I spotted a hole and what appeared to be steps leading down. I started picking my way through the debris, stepping gingerly to make sure the floor held. It creaked in a few places, causing my breath to catch in my throat, but it didn't seem to be in bad shape.

I took a few more steps and heard what sounded like muffled sobbing.

I froze. My heart was pounding so hard that for a moment, I couldn't hear anything above the rush of blood in my ears. Was it possible Edie was here?

I held my breath, straining to hear, but there was nothing besides the groaning of what was left of 88 Spirits.

I must be hearing things, I told myself as I continued to move toward the stairs, although I kept cringing at every step. If there was someone in the basement, they would certainly know I was there, which meant the whole point of my trying to sneak up on them was moot.

There it was again. The sound of a cry.

And it was coming from the basement.

Now that I was closer, I could see the stairs were clear of debris. For that matter, there was also a clear path to the stairs, as if someone had shoved things aside to make it easier to walk through the bar.

Edie was down there. I knew it.

My heart was thudding in my chest, and my breathing was so ragged, I was sure that alone would give me away. Never mind how I had just walked across an extremely creaky floor. The question now was, how would I get down there? Could there be another entrance somewhere?

Or maybe the smart play would be to run back to my car, find a phone, and call Wyle. I could still see Troy's smirk in my head, the way he stood in the doorway with his arms crossed. If he was down there, there was no way I would have a chance against him physically. I didn't even have a stick on me. Just my keys, which I guess if I got close enough, I could gouge out his eyes, but that might be a little too close for comfort.

No, I needed to go back to my car and figure out how to reach Wyle. With any luck, maybe I could also find something to use as a weapon.

I heard the creak behind me too late. I tried to whirl around, but something lashed out and hit me on the head. I stumbled to the ground, trying to protect myself, but instead, I fell into a pit of darkness.

Chapter 19

The first thing I was aware of was the pain.

It felt as if my head were in a vise. Every part of it hurt, from my temples to the back. And when I tried to move, the pain turned white hot and exploded through my skull and down my neck.

The second was that I appeared to be sitting on something cold and damp, with my legs splayed out in front of me and my back against something hard. It smelled cold and damp, as well, mixed with the faint odors of smoke, ash, and snow. Something sharp was poking me under my legs, like I was lying on a bed of nails. It hurt, but not nearly as badly as my head. I also couldn't move my hands or my arms. After a moment, I realized that was because they were tied behind me.

The third was the quiet sounds of sobbing. Along with a strange crunching sound. And ranting.

A lot of ranting.

Oh boy.

I tried to open my eyes, but it was as if they were covered with something thick and gummy. I managed to peel them open and hissed. Even though it wasn't that bright (the only illumination came from the soft gray winter light that filtered down the basement steps and about a dozen candles that were scattered throughout the floor), it still hurt. It was also strangely tinged in red, which made no sense to me.

But I couldn't worry about that right now. The scene in front of me was troubling enough.

Edie was tied to a chair. Her face was streaked with tears, and the coat she wore was not only open, but it didn't look nearly warm enough for the weather. Troy was pacing in front of her, muttering words that I couldn't quite grasp yet. He was the one making the crunching sound, but I couldn't figure out what he was stepping on. Was it ice? I didn't think ice would crunch like that, nor glitter in the dim light of the candles. Speaking of glittering, Troy was carrying something in one hand that kept catching the light. He would occasionally bring it to his mouth.

Oh. It was a bottle.

The brain fog finally started to clear and the pieces of what I was looking at clicked into place. I was surrounded by a sea of broken glass. This was where 88 Spirits had kept their bottles of liquor, and from the look of the things, there had been a lot of them. Not all were broken; a few still stood on a couple of the shelves that were still intact, and others rolled around on the floor, but a lot of them had been smashed. That was what Troy was walking on, as he paced back and forth, his coat hanging open revealing a black hooded sweatshirt and black jeans, his eyes wild.

"You killed her!" Edie accused.

It took me a moment to realize she was probably referring to me, and I would have laughed, except I knew it was smarter for them to think I was still unconscious.

I was a little tougher to kill than they realized.

"I didn't kill anyone," a familiar voice said quickly. It was either Milo or Conrad, but I wasn't sure which one. There were two other figures standing in the shadows on the other side of the basement, but my eyes were still blurry, and I couldn't tell which one was which.

"How can you tell? Look at her face!"

My face? What was wrong with my face? I could feel myself wanting to touch it, but I forced myself to stay still, to keep my expression lax. There would be plenty of time to worry about whatever they did to me once I got both of us out of here.

"She's fine," Milo or Conrad insisted. "Look, you can see she's still breathing."

"Of course she's still breathing," Troy snapped. "I told you to keep her alive. And you would never defy me." He glared at one of the figures, taking another swig from the bottle. "One of you needs to get back on guard duty."

I could see those two exchange a look before one of them melted back into the shadows and toward a ladder that was pressed up against a hole in the ceiling. Was that how they had snuck up on me?

My skin crawled at the thought of them watching me as I picked my way across the bar to the stairs, so focused on how I could get Edie out that I didn't even hear them approach.

"You should still check on her," Edie insisted.

Troy took another drink from the bottle. "I keep telling you she's fine. We only need her for the sacrifice."

Sacrifice? What did he mean by that?

"I keep telling you, there's no need for a sacrifice," Edie said as Troy strode over to one of the shelves that had tipped over. He kicked at it until it broke into pieces, then picked one of the pieces up.

"You know the rules," he grunted as he dragged the pieces toward a larger pile of wood that was situated in the center of the basement. "If we're going to invoke The Forgotten, we need a sacrifice."

"But there's no reason to invoke The Forgotten," Edie said as Troy threw the broken shelf on the pile. It occurred to me then that it sort of resembled the beginnings of a bonfire.

A bonfire …

My dream suddenly filled my mind: trapped in a building, surrounded by fire, and for a moment, I couldn't breathe.

I had to get out of there.

But how?

Troy whirled toward Edie. "Oh, so you love me now?" His voice was taunting, but there was something else mixed in it. Something that sounded like … desperation.

She stared at him, defiant. "I will never love you."

He moved so fast, it was all I could do to keep my mouth shut and not scream. One minute, he was in front of the woodpile, the second, he was slamming his half-full bottle against the basement wall. The third moment, he was in front of Edie, the broken bottle at her throat. "And that is why we're invoking The Forgotten."

I had assumed she would cower, her eyes full of fear. Instead, she simply stared at him, her expression full of disgust. "The Forgotten can't force me to love you."

What? Luckily, no one was looking at me as I struggled to keep my expression neutral. Was that what all this damage and death was all about? Unrequited love?

Troy leaned closer to Edie. "The Forgotten can do anything."

"It can't make me do something against my will."

His eyes glinted in the candlelight as he held the bottle closer to her neck. "You and I both know it can."

"Not permanently. You know it won't last."

He bared his teeth at her as he pressed the bottle against her neck.

"Hey man," Conrad (I was pretty sure it was Conrad) said, stepping closer to him. "Maybe you shouldn't do that. You don't want to accidentally cut her."

Troy whirled toward him, brandishing the bottle in his direction. "What do you know about what I want to do?"

Conrad held his hands up and took a few steps back. "Easy man."

"Yeah, c'mon Troy," Milo said from his spot on the ladder, his voice uneasy. "You don't want to hurt Edie. That's why we're here, right?"

"I know why *you're* here, and it has nothing to do with Edie," Troy snapped, but at least he had moved away from Edie. I could see her take a ragged breath as he went back to gathering wood. But watching him with the bottle had given me an idea. I started to carefully feel around me, searching for a piece of broken glass I could use to cut my way free. I had been testing my bonds carefully, and it felt like tape, so if I could find a large enough piece of glass, I should be able to slice through it.

I found one almost immediately and nearly gave myself away as I accidentally sliced my finger rather than the tape. I gritted my teeth against the pain as I picked it up and tried to maneuver it to cut the tape rather than myself. It wasn't easy, as it was now wet with my blood, but I was determined. Especially every time I caught a glimpse of Troy's eyes and the madness that was barely hidden there.

I was wrong. This wasn't about unrequited love. This was about obsession.

"You know this is all your fault," Troy said as he kicked another shelf to pieces.

Edie looked at him in astonishment. "My fault?" She jerked her hands that were tied with black tape to the chair. "I'm the one tied up here."

Troy eyed her as he dragged another load of wood across the basement. "You should have chosen me. You know we're meant to be together."

Edie closed her eyes briefly. "Troy, we were friends. *Good* friends. Don't you remember those days? When we used to hang out?"

He dumped the broken shelf onto the pile. "I remember," he muttered.

"I used to give you my chocolate chip cookies," she continued. "You used to love my mom's homemade cookies. Do you remember? I liked them, too, but I knew my mom would always have some waiting for a snack when I got home from school. So I would always give you my cookies."

"Because you loved me," he said.

"I *liked* you," she corrected. "I've always liked you. Just like I know you liked me. As friends."

He started shaking his head. "It's more than friends."

"It's not. Honestly. And as my friend, I'm begging you … please don't do this."

He jerked his head up, almost as if she had slapped him. Spinning around to face her, he pointed the broken bottle at her. "What choice have you given me?"

Edie flinched slightly but quickly collected herself. "If you care for me the way you say you do," she said, keeping her voice soft and smooth, "then you'll let Charlie and me go."

"I can't!" His voice was nearly a scream as he shook the bottle at her. "Don't you get it? I *love* you!"

She flinched again. "Troy …"

"This is all Bo's fault. Why can't you see that?"

Bo? The boy in the yearbook picture? The one who looked like the epitome of a bad boy? The one who had died six months ago? That Bo?

Something shifted across Edie's face so fast, I couldn't tell what it was, and then her expression hardened. "Don't you dare bring him up."

"Why? If you had chosen me instead of him, he'd still be alive."

What? I nearly dropped the piece of glass in my shock. Did that mean what I thought it meant? That Troy had killed Bo?

And Bo was the father of Edie's baby?

An awful silence had filled the basement. Even Troy seemed to realize he had gone too far, as he clamped his mouth shut, his expression a mix of shame and guilt. Edie's face had gone completely white, and her eyes were glassy.

"Troy, what did you do?" Conrad's voice was barely audible.

"Nothing," Troy spat as he marched over to one of the shelves and grabbed a full bottle of alcohol and carried it to the woodpile. He tucked the broken bottle under one arm as he opened the new one. "Don't lose sight of what's important. We need to invoke The Forgotten. The rest of this is just a distraction. That's all."

"You think Bo was a distraction?" Edie's voice was high, too high. It sounded like she was teetering on the edge of hysteria. "Bo was your friend! You betrayed him!"

"NO!" Troy shouted as he nearly flung the bottle he was trying to open. "He betrayed me! He stole you away from me!"

"He didn't do anything! It was *my* choice. Mine." Edie's voice was equally loud. She was sitting straight up, her chin high. "I chose Bo! Not you! Never you!"

Troy froze, staring at her, as the blood drained from his face. The whiskey was now spilling out of the bottle he was holding at an angle. "You don't mean that."

"Oh, yes I do." Edie's eyes were as wild as her words. "You aren't fit to say his name."

Troy blinked and seemed to lose himself for a minute, standing completely still as the whiskey continued to drip out of the bottle.

"Maybe we should call this off," Milo said. I suddenly realized he was no longer at his post on the ladder and was instead edging his way toward the stairs. "It's getting dark, and Conrad and I have to work tomorrow, right Conrad …"

It was like a switch flipped within Troy, and his head snapped toward Milo. "No one is going anywhere." He stomped toward the woodpile and started to pour the whiskey onto the wood. "We're here to invoke The Forgotten, and that's what we're going to do."

"But …" Milo started to say as Edie started talking over him.

"You really want to do this? With me here?"

Troy barely glanced at her. "Of course you have to be here. This is all because of you."

She stared at him, her eyes full of disdain, her expression haughty. Something had shifted in her, and even though she was still bedraggled with her hair half in and half out of a ponytail, her face streaked with dirt and tears and tied to a chair, in that moment, there was something queen-like about her. Suddenly, she was the one with all the power in the room. "You really think The Forgotten are going to choose you? With me here?"

He finished emptying the bottle and smashed it against the floor. "Yes, because I'm the one invoking them."

"Not if there's a woman to take control."

He started digging in his jean's pocket. "You wouldn't dare." But his voice didn't sound so sure.

She narrowed her eyes. "Try me."

He almost faltered. I could see it. It was all over his face. Edie had gotten to him. I didn't understand how or what she was saying, but she got to him. And by the looks of the triumphant smile that was tugging at the corners of Edie's mouth, she knew it, too.

But just like that, it was gone. Whatever darkness that was inside him regained control. He gave himself a quick shake and pulled whatever he was trying to maneuver out of his pocket. "Enough of this. We've wasted enough time." And that was when I saw what was in his hand.

It was a lighter.

He flicked it on and tossed it into the woodpile. Almost immediately, the alcohol caught fire and started to burn.

My mouth went dry. My body seemed to seize up. All I could do was stare at the orange and yellow flames dancing on the wood.

My dream. The flames around me. The sound of chanting outside. The curse.

Oh no.

The piece of glass slipped from my hands, and I was even more panicked. My hands were still tied, and now, the glass was gone.

Troy watched the fire for a moment, the flames flickering in his eyes, before he turned toward me. My breath caught in my throat, and all I could do was stare helplessly at him.

He smiled, a cruel smile. "Oh good. You're awake after all." He began to move toward me.

"Troy, leave her alone!" Edie's voice was panicked, but he ignored her, still staring at me. I was straining and fighting with my bonds. I had almost cut through them. It was just one frayed edge holding …

"Troy, I don't think we should do this." Conrad had stepped forward and into Troy's path. Troy barely paused as he reached out to shove him away, but Conrad stayed where he was.

"Really, man. I don't think we should do this," Conrad said.

That got Troy's attention. "You're challenging me? Really?" He sounded almost amused.

Conrad didn't move for a few seconds, and for a moment, I thought he would take control. Surely, he and Milo could take down Troy. But then I saw Conrad's resolve crumple, and he stepped aside.

Troy let out a laugh that had no humor in it. "Yeah, that's what I thought." He continued toward me, his right hand still holding the broken bottle, and his left reaching out to me.

But Conrad had bought me just enough precious seconds to free myself. I kept my hands behind me, but they were lower now, brushing the floor.

And my finger grazed the broken piece of glass.

Troy was leaning down, arm outstretched, when I struck. I pushed myself off the floor and barreled into him. He hadn't been expecting it, and I heard an "oof" as he lost his balance and fell backward. I kept going, driving myself into him, as he hit the ground, and smashed my hand into his open jacket, stabbing the piece of glass into his chest.

For a moment, he just stared at his chest. "You … you …" he sputtered as I crab-walked backward as fast as I could to get away from him. I saw he had dropped the broken bottle, and I scrambled to my feet, snatching it up and holding it toward him as I half-ran, half-hobbled toward Edie.

"Stay away from us," I said, my voice hoarse. I wanted to try to free Edie, but I wasn't sure if I could hold the bottle and get the tape off her at the same time. From the corner of my eye, I could see Conrad and Milo hovering, their expressions shocked. Did I dare trust them to help?

Troy was still sitting on the floor, still staring at the piece of glass. "That hurts! I can't believe you did that to me!"

"I'm going to do a lot more to you if you don't stay where you are." My voice was stronger now and sounded more confident. Far more confident than I felt. I reached out with my left hand to tug at the tape, trying to see if it was loose enough for me to maybe work it off, but as far as I could tell, there was no give.

His face twisted in rage. "You're not going to …" he started to say, but then he was interrupted by another voice floating down.

"Charlie? Is that you?"

My mouth fell open, and I nearly dropped the bottle. Conrad and Milo looked equally horrified. "Mildred?" I called out.

"Oh good. There you are. Is Edie with you?"

Edie? How did Mildred even know Edie was missing? This was turning into a nightmare. There was no way I was in the basement of a burned-up bar trying to protect a pregnant woman with a broken bottle from an insane guy … and *Mildred* had somehow become the cavalry. "How did you find me?"

"I'm a detective! That's what I do." I could actually hear her sniff. "Besides, I saw your car on the side of the road when I was driving around."

Her voice was getting closer to the stairs, and I was starting to panic. The last thing anyone needed was for Mildred to come down here. I could see Troy watching, his eyes bright, like a trapped rat just waiting to sink its sharp needle teeth into me. "Mildred, call Wyle. Right now!"

"Oh, I already did." She was on the top step now. "There's a payphone on the main street. As soon as I saw your car. He should be here in a jiffy, although …" there was a delicate pause. "He's really not happy with you right now."

"I'm sure he's not," I muttered, although at that point, I would have been delighted to see a pissed-off Wyle. "I bet he also told you to stay in the car, didn't he?"

"Oh, he didn't mean it. He knows I'm a trained detective."

Trained, my foot. Although, I had to hand it to her—she did find me, after all.

"Mildred, don't come down here," I said just as I heard the sounds of her coming down here. I eyed Troy, who gave me a long, slow smile.

It sent shivers down my spine.

"Nonsense, I'm coming down," Mildred said, ducking her head and peering into the gloom. "Conrad? Milo? What are you two doing down here? Do your parents know you're here?"

"No ma'am," Milo started to say, but he was interrupted as Troy suddenly launched himself off the floor with a roar, flying toward me, arms wide open.

I grabbed the bottle with both hands, feeling my grip start to slip, and pointed it at him as I tried to brace myself, hoping I wouldn't accidentally fall onto Edie and hurt the baby …

Out of nowhere, Conrad hurled himself at Troy, tackling him to the floor. For a moment, they rolled around as a tangled mess, and it was impossible to tell who was getting the upper hand. But then, Milo jumped in, and after a few moments, they finally had Troy pinned.

Mildred surveyed the scene and put her hands on her hips. "All three of you are in a *lot* of trouble."

Chapter 20

"If you had called me, none of this would have happened," Mildred said as she shot me a disapproving look.

I was sitting at my kitchen table, a pot of tea in front of me, as Mildred bustled around making me more food than I knew what to do with. The crockpot was on as she reheated a pot of leftover homemade split pea soup I had frozen a few months ago, and she was busy hard-boiling a dozen eggs for a week's worth of egg salad sandwiches. When I tried to protest that I was perfectly capable of cooking, she immediately became Ms. Schmidt and told me in no uncertain terms to sit down and drink my tea.

"You heard the doctor," she said as she began slicing tomatoes. "You're supposed to do as little as possible for at least a week to let that concussion heal."

I didn't think making myself a sandwich qualified as overworking myself, but I was too tired to argue. Besides, my head still hurt. If I were being honest with myself, I was glad she was there, prepping my kitchen so I would need to do as little as possible. If this was how I was going to feel for the next few days, I'd be lucky to get myself out of bed, much less prepare any food.

Especially since I knew that once she left, I was on my own.

There was a time when that wasn't the case. There was a time, not that long ago, when Pat would have practically moved in with me. When Wyle would have stopped by "just because."

But that was before I broke my word to both of them and showed up at a burned-out bar to confront a madman who intended on murdering me with no backup, let alone taking a moment to tell anyone where I was or what I was doing.

I couldn't really blame them for being angry with me. It hadn't been one of my smarter moves. But I also couldn't regret my decision.

Edie was alive and safe, and so was her baby. If I hadn't done what I did … if I had waited … if I had tried to go through the "proper channels," that might not be the case.

That had to be worth something.

Right?

"They'll come around," Mildred said, as if reading my mind. She wasn't looking at me, as she was paying very close attention to the tomato, which was probably a good thing. Mildred with a knife in her hand was more than a little nerve-wracking.

I played with the handle of my mug. "I don't know. You heard Wyle."

"Like I said … he'll come around," Mildred said confidently. Way more confidently than I felt.

I could still remember the horror on his face when he first saw me in the basement, kneeling next to Edie's chair while I worked on her bonds, my eyes never leaving Troy as he continued fighting to get free from Milo and Conrad. The broken bottle was on the floor in front of me, within easy reach in case he did get away. The bonfire was still lit, and the wood was merrily crackling away as the flames threw menacing shadows against the wall.

Wyle came first, with two other cops behind him, and he nearly tripped on the stairs in his shock at seeing me. He quickly recovered, his training kicking in, and he clamped his mouth shut, but I could see a muscle twitching along his jaw. He moved closer to us, keeping his gun pointed toward Troy as the other two officers went over to handcuff all three boys. "Are you hurt?" he asked Edie.

"I'm fine," she said. "It's Charlie you need to worry about."

"I can see that," he said, his voice clipped.

"No one has to worry about me," I said. "You're the one who is pregnant. You're getting checked out by a doctor. No excuses."

"Charlie," Edie said in a voice that sounded like she was talking to a three-year-old. "Your face is covered with blood."

Gingerly, I touched my cheek. It felt gummy and sticky. I wondered if that was why I was having trouble opening my eyes.

"You're both seeing a doctor," Wyle said grimly. "An ambulance is on its way, and I don't want to hear one word about it. This is non-negotiable."

The paramedics, however, took one look at both of us and told us in no uncertain terms that we were both going to the hospital to get checked out there. Edie tried to protest, but it was half-hearted. I suspected she was as exhausted as I was.

Luckily, other than some bruises and minor cuts, Edie and her baby were both fine. I had a concussion and needed stitches on a gash on my forehead, but otherwise, I was also fine.

Wyle waited until after I had been stitched up before he came barreling into my room. "What were you thinking?" he hissed. "You knew you were dealing with someone who was incredibly dangerous. Why would you be so stupid to think you could take him down alone?"

"I didn't," I said, feeling stung by his words.

"But that's what you did," he threw back. I had never seen him so angry before, and I found myself trying to back away from him. "You walked into a dangerous situation with nothing. No training, no weapon, no backup …"

"What was I supposed to do?" I cut in. "Edie was with him. I had to do something."

His eyes glittered. "You could have called me."

"I *did* call you. But you weren't there."

He balled his hands into fists. "And you didn't leave a message?"

"No, I didn't leave a message. What was I supposed to say? That I'm going after the guys you were told not to investigate?"

He whipped around, putting his hands on the top of his head as if he were trying to keep it from exploding. Or maybe to stop himself from grabbing me and shaking me. "What about, 'I have an urgent matter to discuss with you. Can you call as soon as possible?'"

"But I didn't want to get in trouble," I said, even as I was starting to feel a little stupid for not figuring that out for myself.

He spun around and glared at me. "Oh, you'd rather I find you dead or severely injured?"

"Well, no. Of course not. But I was just so worried about Edie ..."

"So you didn't think about anyone but yourself," he finished for me.

I felt as though he had slapped me. "That's not true. I was thinking of Edie."

He gave me a hard look. "I thought we were a team. I believed you when you said you were going to back off. No, I didn't think you were going to stop, because I know YOU. But I was sure if something like this happened, that if Edie had been taken, the LEAST you would do would be to call me. The LEAST."

Guilt twisted inside me. I really was an idiot. I should have tried harder to get in touch with him and get his help. "You're right. I'm sorry, but I did try ..."

"Oh no." He started shaking his head as he backed away from me. "Don't give me that. You made a cursory phone call. That's all. And that's not how you treat someone who is on your team."

"That's not true," I said, feeling a little desperate. This was a Wyle I had never seen before, and I was suddenly very worried that I was about to lose him. "I didn't ..."

He held up a hand. "Save it. I don't want to hear your excuses. I have to go." He strode over to the door, putting his hand on the doorknob, but before he turned it, he looked back over his shoulder at me. "I don't know if I can ever trust you again."

And without another backward glance, he left.

Leaving me disoriented and feeling like I had made a very, very big mistake.

"You know how men get," Mildred continued as she started assembling an ice bath for the hard-boiled eggs. "He was upset that he missed all the fun."

Man, how I wished that was what Wyle was upset about. I suspected Mildred knew darn well that wasn't what was going on, but I appreciated her efforts to give me a little hope. Neither of us brought up Pat, whose silence said it all. I knew she would have heard about what happened by now, as Pat ALWAYS knew what was going on. In the past, she would have picked up the phone to call me, or more likely, barged into my house to make sure I was getting taken care of. The fact that she hadn't said it all.

The more I thought about it, the more depressed I got. I decided to change the subject. "You never did tell me why you were driving around in the first place."

She raised her eyebrows in surprise. "I was looking for you."

"But how did you know I was there?"

"Hattie told me."

"Hattie?" Did I tell Mildred about Hattie? I was pretty sure I hadn't told anyone, but now, I wasn't sure. Plus, my head was starting to pound again. The doctor had given me acetaminophen at the hospital, but it didn't seem to be helping. "Maybe you need to start from the beginning."

Mildred gave me another one of her teacher looks. "First, drink more tea. You remember what the doctor said. You're supposed to hydrate."

Obediently, I picked up my cup and took a swallow.

Mildred watched me closely. "More."

What, was I six? Ugh, the price I had to pay for information. I finished half my mug and replaced it on the table. "Better?"

"For the moment," she said as she fiddled with the stove. "It all started with Troy."

"Troy?" I was starting to get confused again. Weren't we talking about Hattie and Edie?

Her head bobbed up and down. "It was really bothering me that I didn't recognize him. I recognize all of my students. I have an excellent memory for names and faces. I kept telling myself that prison changes people, but it still didn't sit well with me."

She brought the pot over to the counter and started transferring the eggs to the ice bath. "So, I started digging into his background. I wanted to see what his criminal history was. It turns out he doesn't have one."

I frowned. "He wasn't in jail at all?"

"Not according to the state of Wisconsin. I couldn't even find evidence of a parking ticket."

"But didn't you say he was expelled? Not that it would mean an inevitable prison sentence, but there would be some record of bad behavior."

"There was no record of that either."

I blinked. "No record of him being expelled?"

She shook her head. "Nope. Nothing at all. Which was really strange, because I know he had been. And I also know he had been in all sorts of trouble as a teenager. Shoplifting, vandalism. I'm pretty sure he even hot-wired a car. But I couldn't find any record of it."

"So if he wasn't attending high school, and he wasn't in jail, then where was he?"

"Sunny Meadows." Mildred's voice was triumphant.

All I could do was stare at her. "Um … what is Sunny Meadows?"

Mildred's face deflated. "Oh, I keep forgetting you haven't lived here very long. Sunny Meadows is a private psychiatric hospital in Riverview. It's very exclusive and VERY expensive."

"Really?" The wheels in my head were turning. "But I thought 1888ers didn't have much money." Although now that I thought about it, the house I had stopped by, the one that was now for sale but had been owned by Troy's parents, was pretty nice. Especially for that area of Redemption.

"That's true, but it doesn't mean every one of them is struggling for money," Mildred said. "There are a few 1888ers who are doing quite well financially, and Troy's father is one of them. In fact, he did well enough that not only was he able to keep his son at Sunny Meadows for years, but he was also able to keep him from having a criminal record."

The pieces were slowly starting to fit together. "Is that why Edie and Hattie didn't want to call the cops? Because the cops had never done anything about Troy before?"

Mildred took an egg out of the water bath and began tapping it on the counter. "It's worse than that. There's a possibility that Troy had something to do with Edie's parents' death."

My jaw dropped. "What?"

Mildred's expression was grim. "It was covered up, of course. Like everything else. I think that's one of the reasons why it's so difficult finding that year's yearbook. It seemed like the school tried to collect them after the fact."

"Why?"

"Because of the coverage of the memorial service. I wasn't able to track a copy down, so I don't know what was wrong with it. Or maybe there was nothing wrong, but the school was just embarrassed about the whole thing. Either way, it sure seems like Troy may have caused the car accident that killed Edie's parents. But Troy's dad, once again, was able to bury it. However, this time, there was a price to pay, and that price was to commit Troy to Sunny Meadows."

"That's horrible. Poor Edie." Again, I saw her in my mind, sitting at Hattie's table, wearing clothes that didn't fit, on the edge of becoming a mother herself … and not having her own mother to help navigate that massive transformation.

Mildred looked as sad as I felt. "I know. It's such a shame. That poor girl." She took another egg out and started tapping it against the counter.

"I know he's obsessed with Edie," I mused as I went back to playing with my mug. "That's pretty clear. But why would he kill her parents? Did he think her parents were the reason Edie wouldn't be with him?"

"I don't know if anyone knows the answer to that," Mildred said. "I'm also not sure when his obsession with her started, but I do know that it escalated. It appears that before her parent's death, Edie had told both the school and the police that she was becoming afraid of Troy. Nothing was done, of course, but it was bad enough that people remembered and did what they could to protect her." Mildred frowned. "Come to think of it, that is probably why the school buried that yearbook. They didn't want any reminder of what had happened."

"The school should be ashamed of itself," I said. While I could at least understand Troy's father wanting to protect his son, the school's part in the whole thing was inexcusable.

Mildred's expression was somber. "The cops were one thing. Everyone knows there's corruption there. This certainly wasn't the first time the cops had botched an investigation or covered something up, and when you combine that with how neither the 1888ers nor the Redemption police want anything to do with each other, I'm not surprised the cops swept things under the rug. But the school …" she shook her head. "I didn't think that was possible."

I wondered how many lives wouldn't have been ruined if they had done the right thing. Edie's, for sure, along with her parents' and her baby's, but what about Hattie and the other community members who had to step up and take care of Edie when she became an orphan? Or Conrad and Milo, who will probably face jail sentences because of Troy? Or Bo, who apparently had also been killed by Troy?

All this tragedy because no one stepped up to get Troy the help he needed sooner.

Speaking of that help …

"Why isn't Troy at Sunny Meadows anymore?" I asked.

Mildred sighed as she fished out another egg. "Troy's dad lost his job, and he couldn't afford to keep Troy there."

"When did that happen?"

"Sometime this summer."

"This summer?" Something inside me seemed to sit up and take notice, but I couldn't quite grasp what it was. "What did Troy's dad do?"

Mildred frowned. "Something to do with finances. Maybe a financial advisor? All I know is he was fired, which is also why he couldn't get another job."

"Which is also why he's selling his house," I said, but I was thinking of something else. There was something there, but my head was still pounding, and it was hard to think.

Mildred snorted. "Well, that and the embarrassment of what his son did. I would sell my house, too."

Chapter 21

"Charlie!" Carol opened the door a little wider to allow me to enter. "You found me! I bet you're here to get paid."

"Absolutely," I said, stomping my boots on the welcome mat before stepping into the foyer. As it turned out, it wasn't all that difficult to find Carol's address after all. It seemed all the 1888ers knew where she lived. I just had to ask.

Carol smiled at me as she took my coat. She looked fabulous, especially when I thought about the Carol who had arrived on my doorstep. Her hair looked freshly styled, as if she had just come from the hairdresser, and her skin glowed. She was carefully made up and wore a soft cashmere sweater in deep burgundy.

Her home was equally impressive. Located right on the edge of where the 1888ers lived, it was a large, two-story home on a well-manicured yard with plenty of evergreens, so it remained green even in the dead of winter. It also sported a large "For Sale" sign next to the curb.

She led me past a tastefully decorated sunken living room with a huge stone fireplace to a large kitchen filled with the latest gadgets and a built-in desk on one side. "I can't tell you how grateful I am for your hard work," she was saying as she waved for me to sit at the oak table tucked into what would be a breakfast nook. "Would you like something to drink before I get your check? I've got coffee, tea, soda. Or, if you want to really celebrate, I have champagne."

"Tea is fine," I said as I gratefully sat down. Even though it had been a few days since I'd found myself in the 88 Spirits' basement, I was still struggling with extreme exhaustion. I gestured toward my head. "No alcohol for me. Doctors' orders."

Her eyes widened. "Oh, of course. Silly me. Let me get you some tea." She hurried into the kitchen to turn on the state-of-the-art stove. "That must have been terrifying for you, confronting The Forgotten. They're a menace. I don't know why the 1888ers don't crack down on them."

"I'm not sure either." I had since learned that the 1888ers had their own ways of maintaining order and getting justice, which was why Hattie told me to call her if I found Edie. I still wasn't exactly sure what that entailed, and I suspected it was better that way. I also couldn't blame them. After witnessing firsthand the way the rest of Redemption, including the police, wanted nothing to do with them, why wouldn't they take everything into their own hands?

"Well, at least they won't be terrorizing anyone else," Carol said with a certain amount of satisfaction as she fetched two mugs and a box of store-bought tea. Inwardly, I sighed. Not my favorite, but there was not much I could do.

"Yeah, it's pretty much an open and shut case." Initially, I had assumed Edie would refuse to testify, but apparently, finding out the truth of what happened to the father of her baby had pushed her over the edge of fear … and now, she was willing to do whatever it took to make sure Troy spent the rest of his life behind bars. I was also willing to testify, but I had a feeling that everyone was going to get a plea deal. "So, I guess that means you can now leave Redemption."

Carol let out a loud sigh. "I can't tell you what a relief it is to get this house on the market. My realtor said she's already getting phone calls, and we'll have our first open house next weekend. Fingers crossed it sells quickly."

"I hope it does," I said as she brought the two mugs to the table, handing me one. "So I guess this means your realtor doesn't think the arson is going to hurt your sale."

Carol settled into the chair across from me, tilting her head. "Why would it? The case is solved."

"True, but with it being Troy … well, that kind of complicates things, don't you think?" I sipped my tea, giving her an innocent look.

Carol was still holding her tea, but she had gone very still. "Why do you say that?" Her voice was careful.

I shrugged. "Well, you know. It's such a coincidence. His father was your financial manager. Such a small world." I let out a tiny laugh.

A muscle twitched in Carol's jaw. "Oh, really? I didn't know that." Her tone was forced.

I widened my eyes, still feigning innocence. "Oh. I just assumed you knew. Redemption being such a small town, and of course, the 1888ers are an even smaller community. Plus, the reason Troy was even here in Redemption was because his father lost his job last summer." I paused as if a thought had just occurred to me. "Wait a minute. Didn't you say that someone embezzled your trust last summer? And wasn't that the same time that Arthur got another investment for his bar?"

Her face darkened. "Arthur didn't get any investment. He's a thief …" Her mouth snapped shut, and with some effort, she smoothed out her expression. "I shouldn't keep you. You're here to get paid, right?"

I nodded. "I am. But I'm not looking for money."

Her face closed down. "What do you want?"

"The truth." I leaned forward slightly. "Why did you do it?"

For a long moment, she simply stared at me as myriad emotions danced across her face. "What are you talking about? I was here when 88 Spirts burned down."

I rolled my eyes. "Oh, come, come Carol. We both know you were here alone and therefore have no alibi."

"True, but that also means you have no proof I was there."

I gave her a slight nod, as if I were conceding the point. "Then there's nothing to worry about, is there? You'll sell your house and move far away from Redemption, and I'll be satisfied because I'll know the truth."

Her eyes narrowed in suspicion. "Why do you need me to tell you anything? You're the big detective, aren't you? Why don't you figure it out?"

I took another sip of tea. "Let's just say I like to have all of my I's dotted and T's crossed."

She didn't answer, just kept staring at me.

I put my mug down. "I don't blame you, you know. I would have been furious. For years, you gave him money to prop up that failing bar, and for him to then *steal* from you? What a betrayal."

"He said since we were married, the money was half his anyway." Her voice was barely audible, and her eyes were distant.

"That must have made you so angry," I said quietly as I carefully shifted to move even closer.

She blinked a couple of times before focusing on me. "You have no idea." Her voice grew stronger. "After all I did for him over the years. All the sacrifices I made. And even after I sat down with him and SHOWED him the numbers and SHOWED him that if we kept going down the same path of me just writing checks, the money WOULD run out, and then how would we live? He claimed that he understood. He said he would focus on turning 88 Spirits around. He said he knew it could be successful. He just needed a little more time, and he would show me."

"But that's not what he did."

Her face had darkened. "He swore it was just a loan. A loan! He stole from me and then tried to tell me it was merely a loan, and he had every intention of paying it back. All he needed was a little more money to get him over the hump to prove it." She huffed out a bark of laughter that had no humor in it. "He even had the audacity to claim that eventually, the bar could support us rather than the other way around. I just needed to give him enough money to get us there."

"Why didn't you divorce him?"

She shot me a look as if I were an idiot. "You don't think I wanted to? He would have bled me dry! There was no prenup. Again, because I was young, stupid, and in love, and it would have cost me dearly."

"So that's why you decided to kill him."

She looked away. "It didn't start out that way. At first, I just wanted to get rid of the bar. I had already gotten that financial advisor fired, although I decided not to press charges. I hadn't completely decided what I was going to do about the bar yet, other than I knew I had to get rid of it somehow, but I figured it would be better if the cops weren't involved at all. Yes, Arthur would be upset for a while, but he would get over it. And without the bar sucking up all his time and attention, maybe we could begin again. We could finally travel without him worrying about being away from the bar for too long. We could go out to dinner and go on date nights or even just watch a movie together. For so many years, I had been convinced that the bar was the real problem in our marriage, and if it disappeared, so would our problems. Eventually I decided the best way to get rid of it was to burn it down."

"When did that plan change?"

It took a moment before she looked at me, and when she did, I let out a gasp, even though I tried not to. Her eyes were so full of venom, they could have singed my skin. "When I realized Edie was pregnant." She spat out Edie's name, like it was poison.

A part of me wanted to get up and walk out the door. Actually, running out the door would be more fitting. Her hatred was so strong that the kitchen practically pulsed with it. But I forced myself to stay where I was and to sip my tea as if nothing was wrong and we weren't discussing arson and murder. "But you told me you didn't think Edie and Arthur were having an affair."

"What, you think I'm stupid? Of course I would tell you that. I'm not a fool. I know the spouse is always the number one suspect. If I had admitted that I knew Arthur was having an affair, that would give me motive."

"So you think Arthur was the father of Edie's baby?"

She sucked in her breath, and some of the rage in her eyes dimmed. "I was sure he was. The way he would treat her. Giving her extra shifts, letting her sleep overnight at the bar. He even gave her money! *My* money! Why would he do that if he wasn't the father?" She clenched her fists so tightly that her fingers turned white. "And he knew how much I wanted a baby. How dare he do that to me? After everything I had done for him over the years … he goes and knocks up a girl young enough to be his daughter?"

"Did you ask him about it?"

"Of course I did! And again, he swore up and down he never touched the girl."

"So how did he explain giving her money and a place to stay?"

She glanced toward me but didn't meet my eyes. "He said she needed help. He wouldn't give me any other details. I was sure he was lying to me, as he had lied about stealing my money. But now ..." her voice trailed off, and I could almost guess the thoughts running through her head. By now, she'd surely heard the truth—that Arthur wasn't the father, and Edie truly had needed help.

"I can see why it would have been difficult to believe Arthur at the time," I said. "After all, he had a history of lying to you."

Her head shot up, and I saw the gratitude in her eyes. "Exactly. It wasn't my fault. He WAS a liar and a thief. He deserved what was coming to him."

I nodded. "No question. How could you have ever trusted him again?"

Her eyes lit up. "Yes! You get it. I knew you would. That's why I chose you."

I kind of doubted that, but I gave her a sweet smile anyway. "Any betrayed woman would. So, that day. Was there a reason why you picked that day to burn the bar down?"

She shook her head. "It wasn't like that. Even though I had made the decision to burn the bar down—I had even bought the gasoline and a pack of lighters that I had hidden in my trunk—I hadn't figured out the when. My plan was to take care of the bar first and then take care of Arthur. I think a part of me was hoping that Arthur might ... well, take care of himself, I guess. I'm not a killer, you know."

"I get it," I said.

"I knew Arthur would be despondent once the bar was gone, and maybe that would be enough for him to ... well, to push him over the edge. Regardless, the bar had to come first, but that was a little tricky as well. I didn't want anyone else to get hurt ..."

"Of course not," I murmured.

"So that meant doing it sometime in the middle of the night after the bar closed. But if I did it then, I had to make sure Arthur was sound asleep, so he wouldn't discover I had snuck out of the house. The problem was that Arthur didn't always fall asleep until nearly dawn, but I didn't want to wait that long, because I didn't want to risk anyone seeing me. For weeks, I was frozen with indecision. Until …" her voice drifted off again.

"Until you weren't," I said.

She stared off to the side, but her eyes were unfocused. "We were supposed to go shopping and have lunch that day. I wasn't lying about that. Even though I was still so angry with him over the affair and the money, I guess a part of me was still hoping he would come to his senses and realize what he had with me. I had given him everything. How could he not have seen that?" Frustration had crept into her voice. "Anyway, it was the same old, same old. He told me he had to work, and I got upset. We fought. He told me I couldn't have it both ways; did I want him to make a success of the bar or not? If I did, he had to work.

"I wasn't happy about it, so he promised to take some time off that weekend to do something with me. I didn't believe him. He was always promising to do something with me, and somehow, it never happened. But I agreed to it. Then, when I was getting ready to leave the house, I heard him on the phone." The rage crept across her face, and her hands tightened into fists again. "It was her! He was talking to his little slut on the side. He wanted to spend time with HER, rather than me. His wife. The one who had given him everything.

"I was so angry, I was shaking. All I wanted to do was scream at him. Instead, I forced myself to leave. I drove around aimlessly for a while before stopping for lunch. It was almost as if I were in a daze. All I could do was think about how he had dared to do that to me. Me, his wife, who had given him everything! Everything but a child." Here, her voice softened dramatically. "But it wasn't my fault. I wanted to give him a family.

"Finally, I couldn't stand it anymore. I drove to the bar to confront him. I demanded to know what he saw in Edie. Was it just because she could give him a child and I couldn't? He told me I was being ridiculous. I asked him if I was being so ridiculous, why was she there with him hours before her shift started? He said she wasn't there, but I knew he was lying. I could see it in his face.

"And I snapped."

She stared at me then, her eyes glittering with a righteousness that made her look like a religious zealot. "He didn't even wait for me to leave. Simply turned his back and climbed the stairs to his office. I assumed SHE was there waiting for him, and just like that, I knew what I was going to do. I went out to the parking lot, making it look like I was leaving, but really, I was just fetching the gas can and a couple of lighters. I also went over to the wooden deck out front, which was falling apart. It had been for years. Somehow, no matter how much money I gave Arthur, he still couldn't find the money to get it fixed. It had been a sore spot between us for years, as I thought it made the bar look cheap, being the first thing customers saw before they even walked through the front door. Ironically, it was a good thing he hadn't fixed it, because it was exactly what I needed."

"Sounds like karma," I said faintly. I didn't want Carol to sense she was really starting to scare me with her complete and utter belief that what she had done was justified and right. But I needn't have bothered saying anything, as she was barely paying attention to me. She was far more interested that she could finally tell someone.

"All it took was one good kick, and several pieces of wood broke off," she continued. "I took one of them inside and carefully crept up the stairs to wedge it under his office door. I could hear him talking in there, and I assumed it was HER he was talking to, but as I was going back down, I accidentally stepped on a stair that creaked. He called out, 'Edie? Is that you? I'm on the phone, just give me a minute.'

"I froze. She *wasn't* in there with him? Then where was she? I searched the bar area, but I didn't see her anywhere. I figured she was probably in the back, which was bad. She could pop out any moment. Even worse, he might try to open his office door before I was ready. I knew I had to hurry. I quickly ran down the stairs and picked up the gas to douse the dining area and the stairs to his office, then lit the lighter and tossed it on the gas. It went up with a whoosh. I was amazed at how fast the wood caught. I then ran to the bar to tear out the phone line before running out. I was halfway across the parking lot when I remembered the extra pieces of wood, so I grabbed one to wedge against the back door. And then I left.

"As soon as I got home, I threw all my clothes into the washing machine, including my shoes, and jumped in the shower. I could smell the gas on me, and I knew I had to get it off before the cops arrived. My coat was a problem, as it was dry clean only." She shook her head in disgust. "My good wool coat! What was I thinking? Anyway, I stuffed it in my dry-cleaning bag and put it in the garage. My car smelled like gas, too, which was another problem. I came up with what was quite frankly a silly story about how I had gotten gas for the snowblower and ended up spilling it on the car and my coat, but I don't know if the cops would have believed me or not, especially since it had been a couple of weeks since I bought the gas. But, as it turned out, I shouldn't have worried. The cops didn't even come by to tell me the bar burned down until it was quite late that night, and it was pretty clear no one was interested in investigating what happened." She rolled her eyes. "I have to say, I never quite believed it when people would tell me that the Redemption police didn't care about the 1888ers, but it appears that they were right."

"That does seem to be the case," I said, even as the voice in my earpiece said, "We got what we needed. We'll be at the front door in less than five."

I gave Carol a genuine smile. "Could I trouble you for a little more tea?"

Chapter 22

"How did you know it was Carol who burned down the bar?" Tilde asked me as both her and Mildred bustled around my kitchen, making more tea and reheating more of my frozen casseroles. I had told them both I was fine; my concussion was healing nicely, and I could truly handle reheating my frozen meals for dinner. But they both insisted, and to be honest, I appreciated the company. Neither Pat nor Wyle had called or stopped by since the day I had come home from the hospital, and I missed them both dreadfully.

"Mildred told me Troy's father was fired from his job as a financial advisor," I said. "It never made much sense to me that Troy would have burned down the bar. At least not if there was a chance Edie was inside. And he certainly wouldn't have blocked the back door so she couldn't get out. At that point, he still wanted her for himself. So, honestly, the only other person who would have wanted Arthur, Edie, and the bar gone was Carol. I knew someone had embezzled from Carol's trust fund last summer, and Arthur also ended up with a windfall of money, so it made sense he would have figured out a way to steal from her. Especially since he wouldn't have considered it stealing."

"I told you it was the wife," Mildred said, bringing over a plate of gingersnap cookies to the table. They were homemade, but not by me, nor Mildred, nor Tilde. Nancy, who owned The Redemption Inn, had baked them for me. My chest hurt as I looked at them, wishing again for Pat's company.

"What I want to know is how you got the cops to set up an undercover operation," Tilde said as she refreshed my tea. "It must have been so exciting."

"A little nerve-wracking, actually," I said, remembering the unholy glee on Carol's face as she described burning down the bar. "But to be honest, I had nothing to do with convincing the cops. The fire department convinced them." I could still remember Officer Capshaw's polite boredom when I told her my theory. She thanked me just as I finished and told me she would look into it. I knew then she wasn't going to do a thing about it. In her mind, the case was solved, and if there were a few loose ends that didn't add up, who cared? Someone was going to jail over it, and that was good enough for her.

It was the nice, good-looking firefighter named Max, who was first on the scene, who actually listened and took me seriously. He was the one who had introduced me to his fire chief, who also had a few questions about the blaze and wasn't getting much help from the Redemption police. They were the ones who had convinced the officers to let me go undercover.

Then, when it was over, Max asked me out. "A drink to celebrate," he said, flashing me a charming grin.

A part of me wanted to. Wyle wasn't interested anymore; he had made that very clear. Maybe a date or two with a handsome firefighter was exactly what I needed to get my head on straight.

But no. Even as I thought it, I knew the answer was no. I tried to tell myself it was because I shouldn't be getting involved with anyone, but I knew that was a lie.

"Just give them time," Tilde said as if reading my mind. I blinked a few times before forcing myself to smile. She gave my hand a quick squeeze before nodding toward the elegant invitation that was sitting on the counter. "Besides, you have a party to look forward to."

"Not just any party, but a Mardi Gras masquerade ball," Mildred said. "It's going to be the talk of the town!"

"It should be fun," I said, even while I was thinking it wasn't going to be fun at all. At least not now. If Pat and Wyle were still talking to me, it would be another story, but now …

"You should start looking for a dress this week," Tilde said. "Because I have a sneaking suspicion that party is going to change your life."

A Note About Charlie's Past

But first, *Masquerading as Murder*, which is book 9 in *The Charlie Kingsley Mysteries* series, is available for preorder and will be releasing at the end of 2026. (And yes, if you have been frustrated with how slowly the relationship between Charlie and Wyle has been progressing, rest assured your patience will soon be rewarded.)

https://www.amazon.com/dp/B0GL9DGB76?tag=michelepariza-20

Speaking of Charlie's reluctance to date Wyle…

You may not know this, but *The Charlie Kingsley Mysteries is* actually a spin-off from the *Secrets of Redemption* series. *Secrets of Redemption* is a 9-book completed psychological thriller series. While it is still clean (no sex, swearing, gore and very little violence) the themes are a bit darker because it is a psychological thriller series.

https://mpwnovels.com/book-series/secrets-of-redemption

https://mpwnovels.com/book-series/charlie-kingsley-whodonit-mysteries

And Charlie's backstory, in particular, is dark. Much too dark to be in a cozy mystery series, which is one of the reasons why I've only teased about her past in *The Charlie Kingsley Mysteries*. (Another reason is that I would be giving away massive spoilers to anyone who wanted to read *Secrets of Redemption*.)

That said, her past is directly connected to why she's reluctant to date Wyle (or anyone really, but especially a cop).

If you haven't read *Secrets of Redemption*, I can completely understand your frustration. As a reader, I would be frustrated with me as well, which is why I wanted to include this note explaining my reasoning along with giving you some options for moving forward.

Option 1: (highly recommended): Read the *Secrets of Redemption* series. It's best if you read the full series in order, starting with *It Began With a Lie*. If your TBR can't handle 9 long books, then you can just read Books 4-5 (*The Summoning* and *The Reckoning*). Those two books are told from Charlie's point of view and are all about how she first arrives in Redemption.

If psychological thrillers just aren't your jam (or if you tried reading *Secrets* and didn't care for it) then you might try option 2.

Option 2: I've created a spoiler-full summary of Charlie's backstory that you can find in my MPW Book Club. You can join for free and get the Cliff Notes version of Charlie's dark past here: https://mpwnovels.com/spoiler-alert-charlies-backstory

However, because it's a summary, you don't necessarily get all the emotional reasons for why she made the choices she did, so I don't necessarily recommend this option. However, I do understand why this might be appealing to some readers.

Keep in mind Charlie's past is pretty dark. She's one of my most complex characters and has made some very poor choices along with some terrible mistakes. If you think knowing this about her might make you think less of her, you might like option 3.

Option 3: Decide what you read in *Masquerading as Murder* will be enough for you.

One of my dark romance author friends was promoting the final book in one of her trilogies, and one of the things she said was the book was very, very dark, maybe too dark for some readers, and if that reader was you, perhaps you might want to consider skipping that book and just know all the characters do get their happily ever after.

That might be the right decision for you in this case as well.

Charlie will address her past in book 9, and maybe what she says will be enough and you can move on with the series.

Or not. (I'll still have the spoiler summary up if you want to read it then, or maybe you'll decide to try the series.)

Whatever you decide, thank you for sticking with me. I know it's taken a long time to get to this point with Charlie and Wyle, and I appreciate the fact that you're still here.

One Final Author Note

Of all my books, *Arson, Old Lace and Murder* feeds the most into my other series:

The Charlie Kingsley Mysteries (obviously): Book 9, *Masquerading as Murder* (where Charlie attends the Mardi Gras Masquerade Ball) is now available to preorder. (Plus, if you haven't read *Murder Among Friends*, that's where you learn more about Fire Cabin.)

Secrets of Redemption: Not only because it's where you learn about Charlie's backstory, but books 6-9 deal with both the 1888ers and The Forgotten.

The Redemption Detective Agency: Also a cozy mystery series, but much lighter and funnier than *The Charlie Kingsley Mysteries*. Mildred and Tilde are the main characters in this series.

https://mpwnovels.com/book-series/the-redemption-detective-agency

You can learn more about all my series, including how they fit together, at MPWNovels.com, along with lots of other fun things such as short stories, deleted scenes, giveaways, recipes, puzzles and more.

Lastly, if you enjoyed *Arson, Old Lace and Murder*, it would be wonderful if you would take a few minutes to leave a review and rating on Amazon, Goodreads or Bookbub. (Feel free to follow me on any of those platforms as well.) I thank you and other readers will thank you (as your reviews will help other readers find my books.)

I've also included a sneak peek of *The Mysterious Case of the Missing Motive* in the *Redemption Detective Agency*, if you'd like to check it out. Just turn the page to get started.

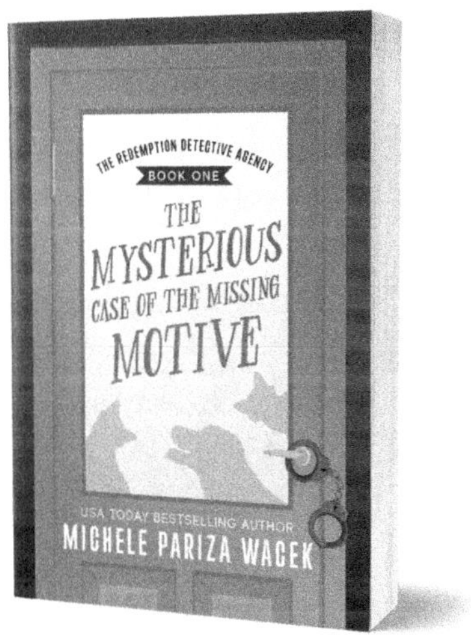

The Mysterious Case
of the Missing Motive
Chapter 1

This couldn't possibly be my life.

There was no possible way that I, Emily Hildebrandt, who graduated with honors from high school and then from the University of Wisconsin-Riverview with a 3.8 GPA ... who, as of ten days ago, had a solid job with a good paycheck, a lovely apartment, new car, and fiancé ... was now sitting in a dirty, smelly bus station in Redemption, Wisconsin, trying not to glance at the clock yet again as I continued to wait for my chronically late Aunt Tilde.

On second thought, I realized I should hope she was just late, rather than having mixed up the time I was arriving. Or the day.

Or maybe, she forgot I was coming altogether.

Oh, dear lord. I scrubbed at my face, torn between laughing and crying.

My Aunt Tilde was a character—crazy, lovable, chaotic. In so many ways, she drove me nuts. She was my complete opposite in just about every way.

Yet … I had always felt a connection with her. She made me feel seen—despite, or maybe because of, her craziness. When I was with her, I felt loved, just as I loved her. But I never felt like I could *live* with her.

Talk about the *Odd Couple*. But worse, because it would be MY life, not a television show.

That said, it was a moot point. No way should I be about to move in with my nutty Aunt Tilde. People like me didn't go through the implosion of their lives and consequent upheaval of everything they've known while being forced to live with their relatives. I was a *responsible* adult. I had done all the responsible, adult, right things. I went to school, studied hard, and picked a useful degree as a business major so I could land a good-paying, solid job … even if it was a little dull. But work is supposed to be dull, right? That's what "being an adult" means—going to work, paying bills, keeping the house neat and tidy. None of these things are fun, but they're all necessary in order to be a responsible adult, like me.

And responsible adults don't need to move in with their Aunt Tilde. Or have their Aunt Tilde give them a job. That isn't how life works.

I must be dreaming. Or trapped in a coma. Otherwise, none of this was making any sense.

If only I hadn't decided to take a closer look at that spreadsheet. Then, I wouldn't have realized something was off. If I had just left it alone, none of this would have happened.

But even as I thought those words, I knew deep down that if I had to do it all over again, I would. Even if it meant losing everything—my job, my home, my car, and my fiancé. Even if it meant I would have no one to turn to except …

"Emily!" Aunt Tilde flung open the door of the station and beamed at me. Her bright-orange hair sparkled in the sunlight and perfectly matched her orange-rimmed glasses, although both clashed horribly with her bright-yellow and red striped shirt. "I'm so sorry I'm late. Traffic was dreadful."

"It's fine. I only just got here," I lied. I seriously doubted small-town Redemption was a snarl of traffic problems, but at that point, I didn't care. I was just relieved she remembered. I got to my feet and started to reach for the suitcase and duffle bag I had tucked under my feet.

But before I could get my hands on them, Aunt Tilde grabbed them. "I can take these if you want to get the rest."

A tight knot seemed to settle in my chest. When I had first moved in with Geoff, my ex, he'd encouraged me to give away most of my belongings. He already had a fully stocked household, so why would we need duplicates of things like plates and towels? Not to mention the apartment was so small, it didn't make sense to clutter it. As usual, he sounded so reasonable, so I ended up selling or donating most of my belongings, including the antique dresser my grandfather had refurbished for me. That, I instantly regretted, along with the set of crystal vases my grandmother gave me as a graduation gift. Now, that regret was doubled. I wondered if Geoff had always viewed me as simply a guest in his space rather than an actual life partner.

I gave my head a quick shake as I reached for the duffle bag. Enough of that. "You don't have to do that. I've got them."

"Nonsense," Aunt Tilde said, trying to juggle both bags. "Go get the rest of your stuff."

A mental image of myself packing what few personal items I had—mostly clothes and bathroom products—flitted across my mind. "This is all I brought. Let me at least take one of them."

I braced myself for questions or condemnations. *What do you mean this is it? I thought you said you were moving here? Who can fit their entire life in one suitcase and one duffle bag?*

But Aunt Tilde just shrugged as she swung the duffle bag toward me. "Smart thinking. Who wants to mess around with a bunch of luggage on a bus anyway?" She started dragging the suitcase to the door, leaving me staring after her in shock.

She paused at the door to glance back at me. "Coming?" I quickly closed my mouth and hurried after her, lugging the duffle bag.

Hot, humid air immediately smacked me in the face as I stepped outside. I shoved a few strands of hair that were sticking to my cheeks back as I increased my pace. For an elderly woman, Aunt Tilde was surprisingly fast, even with my suitcase. "Here we are," she sang out as she approached a light-pink Cadillac that was taking up two spaces, thanks to a very crooked parking job.

I stopped walking, my stomach twisting in on itself. "You have a pink Cadillac?"

She grinned. "I do. Isn't she a beaut?" She patted the trunk lovingly.

Oh no. This was getting worse and worse. "I thought only Mary Kay beauty reps were able to get a pink Cadillac."

"Yep. Isn't it wonderful?" She set my suitcase down and started fiddling with her keys to open the trunk.

This was turning into a nightmare. Was this the job Aunt Tilde had promised me? Helping her with her multi-level marketing business? Was that the reason she was being so cagey about my new job? The idea of sitting in a kitchen surrounded by people I didn't know as I revealed the latest eyeshadow colors was making me break into a cold sweat. "Are you selling Mary Kay?"

She popped the trunk and looked at me like I was crazy. "Heavens no! Do I look like someone who should be giving makeup tips?" She gestured toward her face, which was bare of any color other than a little smeared, pink lipstick, before letting out a rusty laugh. "Good grief." Shaking her head, she turned back to her overflowing trunk.

I didn't move. "If you're not selling Mary Kay, then how did you get one of their cars?"

She waved a hand airily at me. "A friend gave it to me."

A million questions rose up inside me, like how did this "friend" end up with a Mary Kay car? Were they the ones selling Mary Kay? And if they were, why weren't they driving it?

But I forced myself to swallow those questions. Knowing my aunt, I wasn't going to get a straight answer out of her if she wasn't in the mood to give me one. What I needed to do was focus on the positives … like how my mysterious new job wasn't selling makeup, to start. That was a good thing.

Although if I was being honest, beggars couldn't be choosers. Whatever my aunt had in store for me, I really had no choice but to take it and be grateful for it.

And I *was* grateful. Truly. When I finally called Aunt Tilde three days ago, I was desperate and nearly in tears. Geoff had given me five days to pack my things and move out. "And that's being generous," he told me, his voice sounding so reasonable as he explained how, when couples break up, it's customary for one to leave immediately. Of course, in my case, not only did I not have a job, but I also had no money or legal right to the apartment I had faithfully spent every single Saturday morning cleaning while Geoff lazily enjoyed the newspaper and home-cooked breakfast I made. My name was not on the lease, even though Geoff had assured me it was. Not only that, but the so-called "joint" checking account that I had deposited every one of my checks into wasn't actually joint. It was solely his, and I had merely been a signer on it. Needless to say, that privilege had also been removed.

The only money to my name was the twenty-seven dollars in my wallet and $333.96 in my personal savings account that I've had for years. Geoff knew nothing about it. He had promised to send me a check once he deducted my half of the last set of bills, but the whole setup had left me feeling uneasy. I reminded myself that despite all his faults, he had always been fair, and there was no reason for him not to be in this situation. It wasn't like he was a thief or anything. He was just thorough, which was something I had always appreciated about him. I was the same way. And I was sure once he found a few minutes to go through all the bills, he would make it right.

No question.

Unfortunately, though, that meant until I got squared away, I only had access to a few hundred dollars, which wasn't going to get me far. Especially if I had to rent a hotel room. It was 1993, after all … even staying in a cheap, rundown hotel wouldn't last long. Both my mother and sister refused to let me stay with them. Well, to be fair, my mother was the one to outright refuse, which I had expected, although it still hurt. My sister told me I was welcome to sleep on her couch for a few days until I got my feet under me. I had a terrible feeling it was going to take longer than a few days to find a job and an apartment I could afford, though. Between that and the exhaustion in my sister's voice as my two nieces screamed at each other in the background, I knew it wasn't an option. I thanked her and told her I would figure something out.

My friend Deena, on the other hand, immediately offered me her couch for as long as I wanted. "It will be fun, like a sleepover," she gushed. As much as I appreciated the offer, Deena had a small, one-bedroom apartment with a boyfriend who stayed over more often than not. Not only that, but he happened to work in the same law firm as Geoff. While Deena might be fine with me staying with her, I suspected her boyfriend wouldn't be nearly as enthusiastic.

And that's how I found myself standing in a parking lot in Redemption, with the noonday summer sun beating down on my head and sweat dripping off my neck, about to get into a pink Cadillac that I was half-convinced Aunt Tilde had stolen from some nice Mary Kay lady.

When I had called my aunt, there was zero hesitation in her voice as she immediately instructed me to pack up my bags and move to Redemption, where she would not only provide me with a place to live, but a job, as well. I was so grateful and relieved, I nearly burst into tears. Finally, I had somewhere to go that would allow me to lick my wounds and figure out my next steps. I was going to be fine. It was all going to work out.

I should have known there would be a catch.

Aunt Tilde was busy trying to shove my suitcase into her trunk, on top of the mishmash of wrinkled clothes, crumpled fast-food bags, magazines, and cat litter bag, but it wasn't fitting. "Oh, for heaven's sake," she muttered as she tried rearranging things. "Oh, my library books! I need to return them. Emily, can you remind me to do that?"

"Of course," I said, trying not to wince. *Please don't let my job be trying to keep my aunt organized.* Maybe becoming a Mary Kay lady wouldn't be so bad after all.

After a little more pushing and shoving, she finally managed to get my suitcase into the trunk. "Aha! It fits." She turned and gestured toward me. "Here, let's get that other bag in."

I took a few steps forward, still clutching my duffle bag, my eyes fixed again on the bag of cat litter as my stomach filled with a growing sense of horror.

Don't get me wrong … I liked cats. From a distance, and owned by other people. I didn't have any desire to deal with the mess and hair and everything else that came from owning a pet. Plus, I was fairly certain cats inherently hated me. I had been snarled at and scratched by them more often than not, even from the ones whose owners swore were the friendliest around. "I don't understand what's going on with Princess," my elderly neighbor had fretted a few weeks ago when I stopped by to drop off her mail. "She's the sweetest cat I've ever had," she insisted as Princess hissed and spat at me from the corner.

Again, I reminded myself that beggars couldn't be choosers. If my aunt had a cat, I would just have to figure out a way to not be in the same room with it. With any luck, the cat litter belonged to the Mary Kay lady who was now out of a car. "It doesn't look like there's much room. I can just put it in the backseat."

My aunt clicked her tongue. "Nonsense, there's plenty of room. Besides, Sherlock is in the back."

Sherlock? I craned my neck to peer into the back of the car, but as far as I could tell, it was empty. "Who's Sherlock?"

"Oh, she's one of my partners in my new venture," Aunt Tilde said, taking the duffel bag from me and attempting to shove it into the trunk. "You two will love each other."

I glanced at the backseat again but still didn't see anyone. "New venture?" I asked cautiously.

"You'll see," Aunt Tilde answered mysteriously, giving my bag a final push before slamming the trunk shut with a grunt of relief. "Come on, let's get you home."

I followed her to the front passenger side, still trying to get a peek at the elusive Sherlock. All I saw was what looked like a long, black duffle bag similar to mine. Was Aunt Tilde getting a little senile? I didn't think senility ran in my family, but I was no longer so sure. "Aunt Tilde, I don't see anyone …" I said as I opened up the passenger door.

Just then, the head of a feline popped up from inside the duffle bag, and I let out a shriek.

"Emily, meet Sherlock," Aunt Tilde said with a flourish, getting into the driver's seat.

I didn't move. "Sherlock is a cat?"

"Obviously." She patted the passenger seat next to her.

I still didn't move. "And you're telling me this cat is your partner?"

"I said she's *one* of my partners," Aunt Tilde corrected.

"How can a cat be a partner?"

"You'll see. You just need to have a little faith. Now, let's get you home," she repeated.

I could do nothing but look at her in horror. "What sort of venture is this?"

Aunt Tilde beamed at me. "Trust me. You just have to wait a little bit, and then it will all make perfect sense. Now, get in. We need to get going."

Sherlock blinked at me and yawned, revealing rows and rows of very sharp teeth.

What had I gotten myself into?

Want to keep reading? Grab your copy of *The Mysterious Case of the Missing Motive* here:

https://MPWNovels.com/r/baolmmissmowide

Books and series by Michele Pariza Wacek

Charlie Kingsley Mysteries
(Cozy Mysteries)
See all of Charlie's adventures here.
https://MPWnovels.com/r/ck_aom

Redemption Detective Agency
(Cozy Mysteries)
A spin-off from the Charlie Kingsley series.
https://MPWNovels.com/r/da_aom

Secrets of Redemption series
(Pychological Thrillers)
The flagship series that started it all.
https://MPWnovels.com/r/rd_aom

Mysteries of Redemption
(Psychological Thrillers)
A spin-off from the Secrets of Redemption series
https://MPWnovels.com/r/mr_aom

Riverview Mysteries
(standalone Pychological Thrillers)
These stories take place in Riverview, which is
near
Redemption.
https://MPWnovels.com/r/rm_aom

Access your free exclusive bonus scenes from A Cornucopia of Murder right here:

MPWNovels.com/r/q/corn-bonus

About Michele

A USA Today Bestselling, award-winning author, Michele taught herself to read at 3 years old because she wanted to write stories so badly. It took some time (and some detours) but now she does spend much of her time writing stories. Mystery stories, to be exact. They're clean and twisty, and range from psychological thrillers to cozies, with a dash of romance and supernatural thrown into the mix. If that wasn't enough, she posts lots of fun things on her blog, including short stories, puzzles, recipes and more, at MPWNovels.com.

Michele grew up in Wisconsin, (hence why all her books take place there), and currently lives there after spending nearly 30 years living in the mountains of Prescott, Arizona, with her husband and southern squirrel hunter Cassie.

When she's not writing, she's usually reading, hanging out with her dog, or watching the Food Network and imagining she's an awesome cook. (Spoiler alert, she's not. Luckily for the whole family, Mr. PW is in charge of the cooking.)